Jessica smoothed her gown and pulled on her gloves more tightly. She had not remembered the very size of the Varangian estate. She felt almost lost in that immense vestibule where at least twelve liveried footmen stood lining the way to the ballroom, and where maids received the mantles and cloaks of each new arrival.

She had so nearly been mistress of all this. She walked up the red-carpeted steps to the gold and white doors of the ballroom.

This was the worst moment now, the moment when everyone would realize that she was only a guest here. The notorious Miss Jessica Durleigh, the fallen woman who had so brazenly lived with another woman's husband and had had the nerve to return to the town she had so scandalized. Taking a deep breath, she gave her name to the master of ceremonies . . .

JESSICA

by Sandra Wilson

FAWCETT COVENTRY • NEW YORK

JESSICA

Published by Fawcett Coventry Books, a unit of CBS Publications, the Consumer Publishing Division of CBS Inc.

ISBN: 0-449-50083-7

Printed in the United States of America

First Fawcett Coventry printing: August 1980

10   9   8   7   6   5   4   3   2   1

JESSICA

Chapter 1

The sound of the mail coach disturbed the sea gulls and they rose screaming into the air over the coast road. Late evening sunlight turned the wild expanse of heather to a deep pink, and the sea in the bay was indigo.

With a clatter the coach turned at the foot of Harcot Hill, the horses straining on the final stage of the journey from London. The climb was long and the coach moved slowly now. Inside, the solitary passenger leaned to look back toward the bay. In the distance she could see the Welsh coast, a line of purple smudging the horizon. The trees of Harcot Hill slid past the dusty window and she sat back, leaning her head wearily against the horsehair padding. The smell of the sea was clear and fresh and she thought that nowhere on earth was as beautiful and welcoming as Somerset on a warm summer evening.

But would she receive a welcome? She doubted it. She saw the road ahead curving toward the gallows-tree at Hangman's Cross. Only a mile or so beyond lay Henbury, her destination.

She stretched her fingers nervously in their tight-fitting kid gloves. Henbury was her home town, the place where she had been born and raised, and the place she had scandalized by jilting her wealthy bridegroom at the altar to run away with her best friend's husband. Put like that it seemed so very wrong, so very reprehensible. But it had been so right, to run from Henbury with Philip, to cast caution to the winds and spend every hour with him. She toyed with the flounces on her pale blue parasol and her eyes filled with tears. It was all ended now, for Philip was dead. She would never see him again, never hold him close or lie safe and protected in his arms. Blinking back the tears she looked at the stark gallows as the coach rattled across the crossroads and began the long descent to Henbury.

"Well, Jessica Durleigh, you're coming home now," she whispered, staring ahead toward the tall spire of St. Mary's Church rising from the fold in the countryside. They would all know she was coming, for the reading of Philip's will would have insured that. Everyone would know that the notorious Miss Durleigh had been left the cottage of Applegarth and that for some months now it had been repaired and refurnished. They would all be waiting for her to return. She could well imagine the lip-licking glee with which all the old biddies prepared the well-stirred remains of the old scandal, and how they could have poured it all out again and chewed it over until everything had been thoroughly masticated. Well, at least her father was dead now and could not be hurt again by his daughter's reappearance.

She nervously smoothed the dainty muslin skirt of her London gown, picking idly at an embroidered daisy. Henbury was the last place on earth she would have chosen to live, but Philip had left her only a small income and, of course, Applegarth. She had no choice.

As the coach turned a bend in the road she could see Varangian Hall on its cliff overlooking the sea. The elegant Palladian house was bright in the setting sun, its windows glittering as the coach moved along the road. Below it she could see the dark green cloak of Ladywood. Somewhere at the foot of that escarpment nestled Applegarth, although she could not see it. Her eyes slid to Varangian Hall again. Once she would have been mistress of it, Lady Varangian. How would Francis be now?

How would any of them be? Rosamund, whom she had loved since childhood, but who had been so hurt when Jessica had eloped with her husband. Sir Nicholas, Philip's elder brother who had never liked Jessica anyway and who had always had a tender heart for Rosamund. Or Lady Amelia Woodville, Philip's mother, who had so doted on everything her younger son did; except in the matter of Jessica Durleigh. They all still lived at Henbury.

She took a long, shaky breath and composed herself as the coach swayed past the first cottages on the outskirts of the town. Varangian

Hall was hidden from view now by the roofs and walls, and she looked at the remembered buildings fondly. Oh, yes, she could still look gently on Henbury, for she had always been happy there. But in spite of everything, she knew that if Philip were to smile at her now she would go with him again without a second thought.

The cobbles of Market Street were as uneven and pitted as ever they had been, and the coach slowed to a crawl as the horses' hooves slithered on a surface made damp after a recent shower. There was a scent of straw in the air, and the smell of fresh bread as they passed the bakery. She sat back in the shadows as the coach halted at a road junction. Snippets of conversation drifted in through the open window, the soft Somerset voices lying gently on her ears. She saw the apothecary's shop, and Miss Brendon's haberdashery. It was all so exactly as she remembered.

With a lurch the coach moved on again, the guard blowing the trumpet to clear the cluttered road ahead, for Friday was market day and the stalls were being cleared away after a busy day's trading. A dog barked excitedly at the chocolate-and-black mail coach and the coachman cursed roundly as the team jerked nervously. Then they were turning into the low entrance of the Feathers, the wheels crunching and echoing as the coach drew into the galleried courtyard of the old coaching inn.

Jessica held her breath for a moment. She had arrived. She listened to the noise of the inn, watching as the ostlers ran to unharness the tired team.

"Made good time from Taunton then, Ben?"

10

shouted the innkeeper, bringing a mug of ale to the weary coachman.

"Ah, good enough, my friend."

"No sign of trouble over Harcot Hill?"

"Not this time. Reckon as how they're lying low for a time."

"Right enough, for 'tis a terrible punishment they'll have if they're caught. Holding up the Royal Mail be a deportation crime."

Ben climbed wearily down. "Well, they can send the beggars where they likes. I'm for a good feed, a long, long drink, and a good wench to warm my bed for me."

"I can give you the first two, my old friend, but as to the last you'll have to look for that yourself." The innkeeper was grinning as Ben walked past the window where Jessica sat. His smile faded as he saw her.

There was no mistaking Miss Jessica Durleigh. No other woman had that dark chestnut hair and those great big green eyes. He wiped his hands on his clean apron and opened the door for her. "Welcome to the Feathers, Miss Durleigh."

Her heart leapt. She had hardly known him and yet he remembered her. She climbed down, shaking out her sky blue skirts and fastening the buttons of her waist-long jacket. The innkeeper stared at her. It was not often that so fashionable a lady graced his inn, and by all that flew she was a real London beauty now, was Henbury's little Miss Durleigh. But what on earth did she have to come back for? It would do no good, no good at all.

"Pray come inside, Miss Durleigh, and enjoy the hospitality of my house."

"Is Miss Davey here?"

"Tamsin? Aye, she's waiting in the parlor, but I didn't know as how it was you she was waiting for."

The wide green eyes moved coolly over him. "Does your every customer confide in you then, sir?"

He shifted uncomfortably. " 'T was but an observation."

She nodded, walking swiftly past him toward the half-open door of the parlor.

Tamsin waited by the dark fireplace with its highly polished copper pans. "Miss Jessica. . . ."

Jessica took the other woman's hands warmly. "Oh, Tamsin, how good it is to see you again. But you are sure that you still wish to come to me, for if you would rather not then I will understand."

"I'm my own mistress now, Miss Jess, and I don't care what's said. I'll come to you—just as I served at Durleigh Farm all those years ago."

"Thank you, Tamsin, but it will not be easy. Or comfortable. I am not a wealthy woman by any means."

Tamsin's plump country face saddened. "I was right sorry about Master Philip, Miss Jess. Right sorry."

"Thank you for saying that."

Tamsin's face changed suddenly as she saw someone's shadow blocking the sunlight in the doorway. "Oh, Miss Jess. . . ."

Turning quickly, Jessica saw Francis. His hand rested against the door, his pearl-handled riding crop tapping the wood slightly. His golden hair caught the sun as he swept off his tall hat and bowed low to her. His dark green riding jacket

12

was faultlessly cut, as ever, and his breeches clung almost indecently to his hips and thighs. He was every inch the picture of sartorial excellence.

He smiled slightly. "I thought I was not mistaken, that it was you I saw in the mail coach."

She curtsied. "Francis."

His blue eyes rested thoughtfully on her face. "Why have you come back?"

"I am the new owner of Applegarth."

"Ah, yes, the little property which borders my lands."

"I shall cause you no embarrassment, Francis, that I promise you. I wish to live quietly and without moment."

"*You?* In Henbury? My dear Jessica, that will be an impossibility, for Henbury will not let you."

She flushed. "Anything is possible, sir."

"Why didn't you sell the cottage and take yourself elsewhere? I do not mean that unkindly, Jessica, I merely cannot understand why you would wish to come back here after all that happened."

"I cannot sell. One of the conditions Philip laid down was that if I wished to inherit Applegarth then I must promise to live there for two years."

"How like the Honorable Philip Woodville, to make certain of snaring you to his memory like that," he sneered, his overwhelming dislike of his dead rival coming swiftly to the surface.

She drew back. "Francis, I will not listen to you speak like that of him. I loved him very much, and I will always love him. I was once betrothed to you, and I treated you shabbily—I freely admit that I did. But nothing has changed by his death. I will eventually follow him to the grave, and still I will love him."

He smiled again then. "You are so wrong when you say that nothing is changed by his death. So very wrong."

She looked at him. What did he mean?

He tapped his top hat on to his head. "I wish you well of Applegarth, Jessica." For a moment she saw the warmth in his eyes, that same warmth which had been there when he had asked her to marry him those years before.

"This is the first chance I have had, Francis, the first time I have even seen you since that day. I am sorry for what I did to you, for it was none of your fault and you did not deserve me."

He nodded. "I put it down to your appalling taste, Jessica, to have plumped for the Dishonorable Philip when you might have had me. Tut, tut!"

She smiled in spite of herself. "Am I forgiven?"

"Almost. If I forgive you entirely, then I will have no excuse for visiting you."

"You need no excuse, for you are welcome."

"As a friend."

"As a friend."

"Then that is how I shall come, Jessica. The past is past, but I can still find great pleasure in your company."

"You are most gracious, Francis."

"I have little choice, my dear, for to be otherwise would be to be boorish, and a Varangian is never boorish." He flicked his spotless sleeve with his handkerchief, bowing over her hand. "Until we meet again then."

"Good day, sir."

14

"Good day, Miss Durleigh."

For a moment his shadow blotted the sunbeams in the doorway and then he was gone.

Tamsin glanced at her from beneath lowered lashes. "Well, that be a turn-up for the books."

"Tamsin Davey, you'll think nothing, nothing at all. No matchmaking, for I want none of it."

"He've got a soft spot for you still, after all this time."

"No, Tamsin. He said it himself, a Varangian is never boorish."

"I may be a countrywoman, Miss Jess, and never stepped outside Henbury in my whole life, but I knows when a man has a fancy and when he don't."

"Sir Francis Varangian is ever the gentleman, always gentle and polite, kind and charming—which makes my past conduct all the more detestable."

Tamsin went to the window and saw that Jessica's baggage had been unloaded from the coach. "I've brought the dogcart to take us back to Applegarth."

"What's it like there?"

"Oh, 'tis nice enough, more than nice enough. Master Philip had had a lot done before . . . well, before. Shall you have a bite to eat afore we go?"

Jessica looked around the parlor, noticing the two men playing dominoes in a corner by the fireplace. They were deep in their game and she doubted that they'd even noticed the other occupants of the room, but she did not want to stay for all that. "No, let's go. I've seen enough of old faces for one day, and if I stay in Henbury then there's always the chance I'll see some more."

"Ah, maybe you'm right, Miss Jess. I'll bring the dogcart round."

Jessica watched the plump country figure bustle out into the courtyard. She straightened the pale blue ribbons of her bonnet, fluffing them out automatically, as she always did when anxious. Francis she had already encountered. But what of Rosamund? And the overbearing Sir Nicholas Woodville?

The dogcart rattled into the inn, drawn by a shaggy little pony which was so rounded it seemed almost too wide for the shafts. With a long breath Jessica went out to it. Now for the final part of her journey.

Chapter 2

The streets of Henbury were negotiated without
further event, and with great relief Jessica sat
back as they passed St. Mary's Church and went
down the narrow lane toward the ford. The pony
splashed happily through the water and up the
incline between the high hedges of honeysuckle
and hawthorn. The air was scented and in the
hollows there were still some bluebells to be seen.

High above some sea gulls wheeled, and the
sea glinted where the hills parted momentarily.
Then the lane entered the shroud-like, deep green
cloak of Ladywood. The huge forest spread over
the countryside for five miles, from the little bay
below Varangian to the edge of the moor inland.
The wind whispered in the branches that laced
overhead and a blue jay burst from an oak tree

with an excited chattering, causing the pony to toss its head.

Jessica smiled. "It is a world away from London."

"Ah, and 'tis a world you should never have left."

"I loved him."

"And he were married to Miss Rosamund. He weren't for you, Miss Jess, not that one."

"I know. It was wrong. But I'd do it again."

Tamsin raised her eyebrows disapprovingly. "The only good thing you'm left with is the cottage, for when it comes down to it, he've not provided well for you, have he? Eh? Miss Rosamund have inherited the greatest part of his estate, as like she should, being as she was his wife and all. But you, who gave up everything for him, gets left with a cottage, a miserable income, and your memories."

Jessica leaned over Tamsin and drew the reins to halt the pony. "Tamsin Davey, before we go a step further you and I must have something set straight between us. I am back in Henbury, and I am more grateful than you will ever know for your friendship and company, but I will never hear anything wrong said of Philip Woodville. Do you understand? If you cannot speak kindly of him then I pray you do not speak of him at all, for I would hate to quarrel with you."

Tamsin nodded, her pale blue eyes kindly. "Then so be it, Miss Jess, but I'll just say my piece now and have done with it. Master Philip weren't no good, he weren't liked by no one 'cepting yourself and his mother, Lady Amelia. He treated everyone as if they were dirt beneath his feet, high and low alike. Sir Francis didn't like him long

18

afore you came on the scene. Miss Rosamund, well she were made right miserable by her handsome husband, before, during and after your affair with him. His brother, Sir Nicholas, was forever at odds with him over this and that. No one, no one will have been sorry that that last illness took him so sudden. There's just you and poor old Lady Amelia, that's all the souls in this whole world as will mourn for the loss of the Honorable Philip Woodville. Now that's the truth, Miss Jess, take it or leave it. The face he showed to you was not the face by which he was known."

Jessica stared. "You are wrong, he was not as you say."

"Then you go on believing that, for it'll do no harm, like as not."

"Don't treat me like a child. I will go on believing what I know to be the truth. I need no shielding from the world."

Tamsin slapped the reins and the pony moved over along the dappled lane. The birds were singing their hearts out as the last of the evening sun sank toward the west and the topmost branches of the trees were blazing with crimson and gold.

Applegarth stood in shadow when at last the dogcart left the lane at the foot of Ladywood and entered the walled enclosure of apple trees from which the cottage took its name. Tamsin reined in before the front door. "Well, what do you think of it now?"

"I'd hardly know it. When I used to drive past here with Francis on the way to Varangian Hall, I thought how tumble-down and sad a place it was, and yet now. . . ." Jessica looked up at the neat little windows, like sleepy eyes peeping from beneath the new thatch. Fresh whitewash sparkled on the walls, and someone had carefully trained a rambling rose around the little porch so that the clusters of dark red blossoms climbed up toward the bedroom windows above. Away to the left encroached Ladywood, the trees hanging heavily over the crumbling wall encircling the garden. A small plot of vegetables had been painstakingly laid out between the old cider-apple trees.

Tamsin climbed down and pointed toward a path wending its way from the lane, across the grounds of Applegarth, and into Ladywood through a gap in the old wall. "Take note of that path, Miss Jess. 'Tis the old way to the abbey ruins above Varangian Bay, and 'tis more than that. If you hears owt at night, owt strange and uncertain, then you must lie in your bed and make like you've heard nothing."

"Why?"

" 'Tis the smugglers you'll be hearing, and smugglers be no gentlemen."

"Smugglers crossing *my* land?" The green eyes flashed angrily.

"Ah, and they'll continue to do so with or without your permission. There's nothing you can do about it, and nothing you'd want to do about it if you had any sense. Let sleeping dogs lie, they says, and 'tis a sensible maxim to go by in these parts."

"You approve, Tamsin?"

"Do I approve? What sort of question is that? Of course I don't, but then I value my neck and all, so I lies nice and quiet in my bed of nights and I says and does nothing when I hears those donkeys pass by towards the abbey. Now, let's go in and I'll brew a pot of tea and set out something for you to eat."

Jessica climbed down from the dogcart and turned Tamsin's key in the lock of the yellow door. She stepped directly into the kitchen with its red-raddled floor. The air smelled of the paraffin with which Tamsin had polished the panes of the latticed windows. Onions, dried mushrooms, and apples hung in strings from the beams and a smoked ham swayed in the breeze from the doorway. Brass and copper utensils hung on hooks and rested on countless shelves around the newly-installed range that was surely the height of modern fashion in Henbury. Above the chest stood a row of pewter mugs and next to them two oil lamps, shining and polished. Some small hoggins completed the shelf, their caps arranged neatly beside them. On the scrubbed table was a clean napkin, beneath which Jessica found some newly-baked Banbury cakes. She picked one up and bit into it, savoring the melting pastry and the spicy taste. It was a taste that took away the years and she was a little girl again, standing in a farmhouse kitchen watching Tamsin roll out pastry with floury hands.

She listened to Tamsin leading the little pony around to the small stable behind the cottage, then licked her fingers before taking the copper kettle to the hand pump over the stone sink. The range had been blackened lovingly, and Jessica smiled at her own reflection in the metal.

The kettle was just beginning to sing when

Tamsin came in at last, carrying a single hand case. "The rest can wait till morning light, it'll be safe enough in the stable. Have you looked around?"

"No, I've only been admiring your kitchen."

"Then look through here. This was how Master Philip left instructions the drawing room was to be furnished. He decided upon the bedroom upstairs as well." Tamsin's pleasant face reddened slightly and she quickly opened the drawing room door and Jessica stepped inside to look.

Her first impression was of chintz: chintz curtains, chintz covers on the chairs, and colorful cushions. The floor was of dark wood, stained and polished until the curtains and covers were reflected in it. Beneath a window stood a huge carved chest, and a table and chairs stood at the far end of the room away from the fire. In the empty fireplace rested a huge china bowl of roses, and Jessica could smell their perfume wafting on the draft from the open window. It was a homely room, comfortable and practical and at the same time completely in keeping with the cottage—yet not in keeping with Philip's taste. She thought it strange that he should have chosen to furnish and decorate the room in such a way.

Tamsin was carving some cold meat as she turned back into the kitchen.

"Philip chose it?"

"Ah."

"And the bedroom?"

"Ah, and the bedroom."

Cool air rushed down the stair well as she opened the door and began to climb. The large landing was simply furnished with Tamsin's few belongings, but the single bedroom beyond was a surprise that caught Jessica's breath. The four-poster bed was hung with dark mulberry brocade and golden tassels, and the coverlet was of the softest swansdown. Chinese wallpaper of pale pink silk threw a gentle warmth over the room—a warmth picked up by the deep rose curtains at the tiny window. Ruby, mulberry, and white rugs were scattered on the dark polished floor, their fringes carefully combed and straightened and their pile fluffed by Tamsin's industrious brush. Unlike the drawing room below, this room spoke of Philip Woodville's taste. She crossed the room to rest her hand on the carved oak post of the bed, her eyes lowered to the mulberry drapes; mulberry had been his favorite color. He was so easy to recall, she thought, so very easy, with his thick dark hair tousled and his cravat awry, and a smile on his lips as he held his hand out to her. Suddenly Applegarth seemed empty and lonely, just as her life now was.

The sound of a heavy coach passing down the track behind the cottage drew her attention to the window. Through the small panes she could see the matched team of grays moving slowly down the incline from the direction of Varangian. She stared at the remembered Woodville crest on the coach's paneling, and with a jolt met the eyes of the woman inside. Rosamund blinked, her lips parting in surprise as she saw Jessica's figure, and then with a snap she drew down the coach's blinds.

Jessica sat disheartened on the bed, her hands clasped in her lap. Rosamund would never forgive her for the past, never. Already the two

23

years she must spend at Applegarth seemed a lifetime, a life sentence. She was jolted from her thoughts by Tamsin's voice calling her down to the kitchen.

Chapter 3

That night she lay awake in the mulberry-draped bed, staring up at the golden tassels that moved in the breeze from the open window. She could see the sky above the dark mass of Ladywood, the stars bright and as clear as cut diamonds, but there was no moon. Tamsin had warned her that tonight the smugglers would go through the woods to the bay. Moonless nights were always good for their activities, for the revenue men would not see so easily, nor would Sir Francis' gamekeepers who were out watching for poachers.

The single bray of a donkey made her sit up. Gathering her dressing gown around her she slipped from the bed and tiptoed past Tamsin's little bed on the landing. The stairs creaked as she descended, but then from the kitchen window she could look out across the orchard toward the path into Ladywood.

The donkeys moved slowly, black shapes of no depth, and silent but for that one earlier sound. The men were as indistinct as the beasts they led, and she found she was holding her breath until the last donkey had vanished through the break in the old wall and into Francis' woods.

She knew her next action was foolish but she could not help herself. Quietly she unbolted the door and went out into the cool night air. The wind rustled the trees and somewhere an owl called. The stars winked and flashed and the air was full of the scent of roses. Beneath the apple trees the grass was damp, dragging at her night clothes as she walked beside the path toward the opening into Ladywood.

The trees stretched beyond the boundary of her land, their leaves whispering secretly and the air wafting more coolly from depths of the wood, as if rushing up from the foam of the waves on the distant beach. She could see the path running straight until the deep shadows swallowed it. For a moment she hesitated, for to go on would be more than the height of foolishness, yet curiosity pushed her to follow the smugglers who so brazenly used her land to come and go. She stepped over the crumbling, fallen stones of the wall and she was in Ladywood.

She had not seen the horse. It was tethered close to a holly tree, its dark glossy coat mingling with the shadows so well as to make it almost invisible. It was the slight jingle of its harness that caught her ear so that she froze, her hand in the very act of brushing aside a low-hanging branch.

She heard the shouts from deep in the woods, and through the tangle of trunks and branches she could vaguely see bobbing lights. Hounds began to bay and the donkeys brayed nervously. Jessica stared, her eyes round and her heart thumping. She turned, stumbling back towards the gap in the wall, but there was a sharp click and she was brought to an abrupt standstill as her trailing hem set off a trap. The fierce metal teeth closed over the folds of material and she was caught.

With a cry of dismay she crouched to try to drag the ugly teeth apart, but it would not budge. Desperately she struggled with it, trying to lift the trap itself, but it had been chained to a tree and she was held fast. Her only escape would be to remove her clothes. She looked toward the bobbing lights, they were coming nearer now and she could hear men running towards her.

The horse whinnied nervously and she turned. A man in a heavy cloak was untethering it. Jessica shrank into the shadows but he had seen her. He came quickly over and she stared at him. "Sir Nicholas?"

Philip's brother glanced up from the knife he had drawn. "Miss Durleigh," he said, his polite, disciplined voice so out of place in the alarm of the moment. The knife cut through her skirts like a flame through butter and she was free.

He pushed her roughly towards the path. "Get back to Applegarth, and be quick about it." The noise was redoubled in the woods and a pistol was fired. Nicholas frowned, his dark face reminding her poignantly of his dead brother. "God curse Varangian," he muttered, seizing his horse's reins.

And then he was gone, mounting the nervous beast and urging it along the path into Applegarth. She followed, watching with a mixture of amazement and anger as he rode thoughtlessly across the few vegetables that Tamsin had planted beneath the apple trees.

Gathering her cut, soiled skirts she ran toward the cottage, throwing open the door and shutting it quickly, pushing the bolts across firmly. Tamsin hurried down the stairs in her voluminous white gown, a nightcap set at an angle on her plaited brown hair.

"Miss Jess? . . ."

"Hush, Tamsin. Look, there they are!" Jessica pointed through the window at the men running from Ladywood. They ran swiftly, their bodies bent. There was no sign of the donkeys, but the lights bobbing through the trees were closer than ever and the hounds were giving deep voice as they pursued the smugglers.

"Miss Jess, you didn't go out there?"

Jessica nodded rather shamefacedly, for she could not understand her own foolishness.

"After all I'd warned you!"

"Shh. Look."

At the edge of Ladywood the lights had halted. They could see the men's faces by the light of the lanterns and how hard it was to control the straining hounds that still sought to follow the scent. A man on horseback appeared behind the others, moving slowly through the gap in the wall into Applegarth. He controlled the nervous horse expertly, and Jessica had no trouble in recognizing Francis.

She held her breath as he stared toward the cottage. Would he come to the door? She brushed her skirts nervously, for although she could remove the stains, how could she conceal the great cut where Nicholas Woodville's knife had freed her?

Then Francis turned back to his men and they melted back into Ladywood, the lights gradually vanishing among the trees. Only the constant sound of the hounds told that they were there.

Tamsin lowered the blue and white curtain and turned to Jessica. "Whatever possessed you, Miss Jess?"

"I don't know, and that's a fact. I saw them going in and felt the urge to follow. Oh, don't say it again, Tamsin, for I know I should not have done it!"

"But what happened to your clothes? Did they catch you then?"

"No. No, I stepped against a trap and it caught my hem." Jessica stared at the sliced-through cloth.

"Then how did you get free?"

"Sir Nicholas Woodville freed me."

"Sir Nicholas? But what were he doing there?" Tamsin stared at the window as if seeing into Ladywood.

"I don't know. His horse was tethered just inside Francis' lands, and he seemed in a veritable anger about Francis' men falling on the smugglers." She glanced at Tamsin as she realized what she was thinking.

29

"Miss Jess, do you think Sir Nicholas be the leader of the smugglers?"

"I don't know. I really don't know. He was there, certainly."

"Well, I never. They reckon hereabouts that someone of the gentry must be leading the ring, but no one outside the ring itself is in the know. But Sir Nicholas Woodville?—that be a hard pill to swallow, him being so upright and strict to the letter of the law. A right turn-up that would be, and no mistake."

"We don't know that that was why he was there, Tamsin, so don't go jumping to any conclusions."

"Oh, I shall say nothing. I'm no daft curmudgeon to go sounding my tongue foolishly. Nonetheless, 'tis a strange happening, a real strange happening."

"Tamsin, let us have another pot of your excellent Formosa tea."

"Reckon us'll sleep 'till noon tomorrow."

"It doesn't matter if we do."

"That's true enough."

The kettle was singing happily on the range when Tamsin set the pretty blue and white crockery on the table. "Miss Jess, did you see the Woodville coach earlier?"

"Coming down from Varangian? Yes. Rosamund was in it."

"Ah, that's what I were coming to. 'Tis whispered, only whispered, mind, that Miss Rosamund do have her heart on her sleeve for Sir Francis."

Jessica stopped toying with her spoon and looked up swiftly. "How much of a whisper is it?"

"That's neither here nor there, if 'tis a whisper then 'tis suspect. She do spend some time over there, and that's no whisper. Mind, *I've* always thought it were Sir Francis as she loved, and never Master Philip, but her folks wanted the Woodville marriage and anyway, Sir Francis had his heart set on you."

"Your instincts are nearly always right, Tamsin, and if you think she has always loved Francis then I am prepared to believe that it is so. But does Francis love her?"

"Him? I doubt that if he did he would let her know. First off she were Master Philip's wife, and now only recently widowed. He'd not make so low as to express his feelings one way or the other. He'm a gentleman through and through, a *proper* gentleman, not like some others as come to mind."

Jessica flushed. "The kettle's boiling."

"Ah," muttered Tamsin enigmatically.

The kettle's lid was rattling as steam billowed out. The tea hissed pleasingly in the silver teapot and Tamsin sat down while it brewed.

"Miss Jess, I know as it's none of my concern, but now seems as good a time as any to say what's on my mind. Sir Francis loved you once, and today at the Feathers it seemed to me he was still smitten. Perhaps it was just his way, but nonetheless, that's how it looked. Now, Miss Rosamund loved him those years ago when you jilted him for Master Philip. She saw Sir Francis hurt by you and she saw her own husband desert her for you. As if that weren't enough, you now come back to Henbury and already you've been talking with Francis again. She'll see you as a threat all over again. I beg of you, Miss Jess, stay

31

well away from her, for any meeting 'twixt the two of you will only be painful—and you'm the one as'll be hurt the most for she've got right on her side. You didn't then and you haven't now."

"But I don't want Francis."

"It don't matter what you want now, it's how she's going to see it that counts."

"Two years is a long time, isn't it?" Jessica's green eyes were dark in the light of the candle Tamsin had set on the table.

"Well, less'n you want to go to the poorhouse, Miss Jess, two years is what you must live here for. The sooner it passes the better for all concerned. Now then, drink this and then we can get us back upstairs to bed." Tamsin frowned at the cut hem again. "That great, foolish man, cutting it like that. It be spoiled beyond redemption!"

Jessica sipped the tea, thinking of what Tamsin had told her and thinking, too, about the strange affair of Sir Nicholas Woodville and the smugglers.

Chapter 4

The sun was warm as Jessica walked slowly along the track above Applegarth. Ladywood was noisy with the singing of birds and now and then she heard the lazy humming of bees among the foxgloves that bloomed among the ferns. She would not go much farther now, just to the brow of the hill above Varangian to see the sea.

She twirled her parasol, watching the twisting shadow on the road before her, and breathing deeply of the scented Somerset air. Everything was so sweet and warm, so much as she remembered it. A tubby black and white puppy erupted from the ferns close by, yapping and capering around her as if fit to burst.

"Nipper!"

She turned as a young man carrying a shepherd's crook came from a hidden path calling the mischievous, disobedient puppy to heel.

"Good morning, miss, I'm sorry if he frightened you."

She smiled, liking his pleasant look and friendly brown eyes. "He didn't frighten me, he's a little small to do that."

"He's full of his own importance this morning, for he's had his first working with the sheep."

"Whose sheep?"

"Sir Francis'—I'm his chief shepherd now my father's dead and gone."

"You must be Jamie Pike then!"

"Yes, miss." He looked puzzled, "How? . . ."

"You don't remember me do you? And yet once we sat next to each other in church and you pulled my hair until I scratched you and we were both chided in front of the whole congregation."

His eyes cleared. "Miss Jess! Well, I'd not have known you. My, you're the fine lady now right enough."

"Not really. I'm still Jessica Durleigh. I'm no different."

He grinned. "That's hard to swallow when I look at you." He indicated the crisp brown and white gown and bonnet and the dainty white slippers peeping from below the frilled hem of the gown.

"They say you should not tell a book by its cover, and so I look at you in your rough old clothes and needing a good wash, and I say to myself that it is hard to remember that Jamie Pike had the sharpest tongue and mind in Henbury and that even as Sir Francis' shepherd you are wasting your talents."

His eyes were steady. "I'm happy like this."

She raised her eyebrows. "Perhaps you are. I wouldn't know."

Nipper began to bark suddenly, staring up the hill to the summit. A smart scarlet curricle skimmed over the brow from Varangian, its team clipping briskly at the expert touch of the driver. The whip cracked as Francis brought the horses in a spanking pace along the hilltop and then down the incline. Nipper was almost beside himself as the bright red object hurtled toward him, its two large wheels crunching on the little stones and pebbles.

"Nipper!" Jamie called urgently, but the puppy cavorted in the middle of the track.

Francis seemed not to have seen it, for the whip cracked again and the horses' hooves clip-clopped more swiftly. Jessica ran forward, beating at the surprised and indignant puppy with her parasol and knocking him head over heels into a clump of foxgloves. Then she stumbled in a rut and almost fell beneath the hooves of the team that reared and nearly upset the curricle.

Winded, she lay there, her brown and white gown ripped and her bonnet tipped forward over her eyes, the ribbons slithering undone. Nipper recovered his aplomb and bounced from the foxgloves, snarling and snapping at the ribbons as if he would like to shake the life from them. Gritting her teeth Jessica snatched her parasol and clouted the pup. "Oh, go away, you stupid beast! Go and chase your tail somewhere else!"

Jamie stood rooted to the spot, his eyes moving from Jessica to Francis.

At last the team calmed sufficiently for Francis

to climb down and tether them to a tree. They shuffled a little, their eyes on the puppy, but Nipper was cowed at last and his tail was between his legs as he slunk back to Jamie.

"Pike! Is that creature yours?"

"Yes, Sir Francis."

"By all that's holy! You've not had your position with me for long, and you'll lose it if you go abroad with so unruly a beast again." Francis reached down to help Jessica to her feet. "Are you all right?"

"Yes. I fear my dignity is ruined though." She glanced down at the rip in the brown and white muslin with a rueful smile.

"Permit me to take you home, if you will trust my capabilities after so near a disaster."

"Oh, I am certain that you are quite the tippy with the ribbons, good sir." She laughed.

His smile faded a little. "I do not like to hear such foolish society tattling on your lips, Jessica."

"And I do not like being corrected by you, Francis."

He nodded. "I asked for that. Shall I help you into the curricle?"

She placed her hand in his and in a moment was perched in the high seat behind the two bays. He nodded peremptorily at Jamie who still stood at the roadside, cap in hand. Nipper sat by his feet gazing at the curricle with soulful, melting eyes.

Francis climbed beside her, flicking the whip a little. The horses moved away and the curricle swayed alarmingly on its large springs. Francis glanced at the cloak of trees on either side. "It's another dark night tonight," he said, glancing at her.

"You are thinking of the smugglers?"

"Yes. They use the path across Applegarth, you know."

"I know. I saw something of what happened last night. Is there nothing to be done to stop them?"

"Only rebuilding the wall, but that would merely cause them to enter Ladywood elsewhere."

"Then why do the revenue men not wait just inside the wood and capture them when they come with the donkeys?"

"Half the revenue men have a vested interest in the smuggling. There is much corruption, I fear."

"And you risked yourself and your men trying to capture them last night?"

He laughed. "Would that I could look noble and admit that to be so, but I fear I was merely looking after my own interests. I was seeking poachers, not smugglers, and fell upon the wrong villains. The poachers in the meantime made off with several fine deer that, no doubt, rest in secret places in the churchyard of St. Mary's right now, awaiting collection."

"Then watch the churchyard if that is so."

He shook his head. "No. I would not do that. They are hungry and cannot give their families a good Sunday meal. If I can catch them before they get the game from my lands that is one thing, but after that they may keep it. I've more than enough for my purposes. It's the nerve they display which draws me, I fear."

"And the thrill of the chase when the quarry is crafty enough to think for itself."

His smile broadened. "Perhaps. You are too astute, my dear Jessica."

As they emerged from the trees above Applegarth he slowed the team to a walk. "Do you recall the summer ball held each year at Varangian?"

"Yes, it was always quite the thing to cadge an invitation."

"An invitation has been set aside for you."

"No. No, I could not come, Francis. I know you mean well, for you are kind. But I am most definitely *persona non grata* in Henbury society."

"If they wish to forego their annual banquet that is their affair. I would like you to come. I think they will choose to smile at you at Varangian rather than miss the high point of the social calendar. And once they have done that, then they can hardly ignore you in Henbury market square, can they?"

"You don't know them very well, do you? They would snub me if it pleased them to do so."

"I shall send the invitation nonetheless."

"I do not know that I shall accept."

He maneuvered the team into Applegarth and she saw with a start that a black horse was tethered outside the front door. Sir Nicholas Woodville was paying her a visit.

"I see you have a visitor." Francis' eyes searched her face for a moment."

"I cannot think why Philip's brother should wish to see me."

He helped her down from the curricle and for a moment she held his hand. "Do not invite me to the ball, Francis. For Rosamund's sake I will not come."

"Rosamund? She did not even like Philip Woodville, so why should she concern herself about your presence at the ball?"

"Oh, Francis! Why are men always so very dense over these things? Suffice it that I will not come and that Rosamund would prefer it that way."

She released his hand and went into the cottage.

Chapter 5

Tamsin looked up from the table where she was pounding dough as if she had a grudge against it. "Miss Jess, what have happened this time?"

Jessica looked at the ripped gown again. "I fell. Is Sir Nicholas here?"

"In there, drinking that there Madeira as if we had a well of it."

"Did you lace it well with tansy?" asked Jessica in a soft whisper, a wicked grin on her face.

"Would that I had, for I'd relish each gripe he felt, great, overbearing so-and-so that he is."

"I'd better see what he wants. Did he give any hint?"

"Not a word, nor would he to the likes of me." Tamsin sniffed angrily and thumped the dough again. "Proper ruffles my feathers he do!"

"And mine, if he did but know it."

Jessica took off her bonnet and laid the parasol on a chair. "Do I look too bad?"

"No, there's only the tearing now. You looks fit for Carlton House itself and the company of the Prince Regent."

"That's all Sir Nicholas would say I am fit for anyway." She lifted the latch of the drawing room and went in. "Sir Nicholas?"

He stood, bowing slightly. "Miss Durleigh."

With some amusement she noticed that his tone was exactly as it had been the night before in the woods. She looked at him. He was so like Philip, only older. But there was none of Philip's softly handsome looks about this last remaining Woodville son. Nicholas' face was good-looking, but stern; his hair was dark and curly, but with a touch of gray here and there; and his figure, although elegant, was not as slender and graceful as had been Philip's. And there was a coldness in his eyes that chilled her.

She crossed the room and sat on the wooden, high-backed settle, her back straight and her hands folded in her lap. "What brings you to Applegarth again, Sir Nicholas."

His eyes flickered. "Matters of great import, Miss Durleigh."

"Perhaps you wish to replace the peas which your horse trampled last night."

"Peas?" He looked blank.

"Yes, sir. Peas."

He straightened his crisp white cravat uneasily. "I saw no peas, madam." With a flick of his dark green coattails he sat down opposite her. "I will, of course, have my gardeners send over fresh plants if I am indeed guilty of riding over yours."

42

"Will they not wonder how it came that you rode over my garden in the middle of the night?"

His eyes were steady then. "Or how you were out in your night clothes creeping around Ladywood?"

"Perhaps we should forget the peas."

"Indeed. Now, Miss Durleigh, believe me that I would not have come here at all were it not so important."

"I am listening."

"My late brother was a reasonably wealthy man, you will agree, but in no way was he sufficiently well off to live as he did."

She colored slightly. "I do not see why this concerns me."

"What I must ask you is this. Do you know of any business ventures, investments, gambling successes, or anything that would account for this seemingly vast fortune he had access to?"

"No. Sir Nicholas, are you suggesting that Philip was in any way dishonest?"

"I suggest nothing. I merely seek to know the truth. I cannot help having noticed on going through his papers, that there were bills and receipts for large sums of money, far more than his income from the family. I know you are no great heiress, Miss Durleigh, and neither was Rosamund, and I know Philip's legitimate income. I can find no hint of how he became so wealthy."

"If Philip had wished you to know, then he would have confided in you. So, even if I did know, I would certainly not tell you."

He seemed unruffled. "Then I assume you do not know?"

"No, Sir Nicholas, I do not know. I was, as you

well know, your brother's mistress, not his business associate. We shared a bed, not an account book."

"I see no reason for coarseness, Miss Durleigh."

"Do you not? Then you astound me still further, sir."

"I'll grant that I perhaps warrant the sharp edge of your tongue, but believe me I have not come here to cause you upset. I am genuinely concerned about this money."

"But why? It cannot have any bearing on your affairs."

"Because my family's accounts and books are shortly due for audit."

She stood then. "You think Philip embezzled the money from your family? How *could* you?"

"It is a possibility, Miss Durleigh. I merely seek to cover all possibilities."

"Philip would never do such a thing, never!"

He rose, bending to pick up his top hat and riding gloves. "I fancy that even after all this time I was more aware of my brother's character than you. He treated you like a princess because he loved you and because he did not want you ever to discover how unpleasant he could be. Everyone else in Henbury knew the truth of how loathsome dear Philip was at times. Even my mother knew, although she still won't admit to it."

"Good day, Sir Nicholas!"

"There is just one more thing. Do you know anything of this?"

He set a folded sheet of paper on the table before her. It was a receipt from Slade's, the jewelers of Bath. She blinked, for it concerned a

44

diamond necklace—the price of which took her breath away. "I know nothing of it," she said stiffly. "Now please leave Applegarth."

He gathered the receipt and hesitated for a moment. "Miss Durleigh, now that I have made myself thoroughly odious in your eyes, I fear I must ask yet one more thing of you."

"What?"

"It concerns last night."

"Yes?"

"I would prefer it if no one came to hear of my presence in Ladywood."

She stared at him. "I have told only Tamsin."

"And nothing will go any further?"

"If that is your wish, sir."

"Thank you, Miss Durleigh. Good day."

"Good day."

She listened to his footsteps crossing the tiled floor of the kitchen, and the sound of his horse leaving Applegarth. She sat back down on the settle feeling a little unsteady. Why was everyone so unpleasant about Philip? Tamsin, Francis, and now even Sir Nicholas. Why?

Chapter 6

The summer evening was long and pleasant.
Jessica sat back on the grassy bank above Applegarth, looking across the valley toward the spire
of St. Mary's in Henbury. The shadows were
lengthening now, but the air was still warm and
she could hear the droning of insects beneath the
low-hanging branches of a beech tree. Down in
the cottage the kitchen window glowed with the
light of a lamp and she could see Tamsin inside
testing a flat iron before embarking upon the
repair of the brown and white muslin gown.

It was so pleasing to sit there twirling a blade
of grass between her fingers that Jessica was
loath to stir herself. She lay back among the
dancing grasses, looking up at the lacework of
soft green leaves overhead.

Jamie emerged stealthily from the woods a little to her right and she saw him immediately, but something in his manner made her remain silent, watching him as he made his way quickly and quietly down the slope to vanish into the small stable. She heard the snorting whinny of the pony and then nothing more. Undecided, she lay watching. What was Jamie Pike doing so secretly?

He slipped from the stable as silently as he had come and Jessica lay as if she would hide beneath a willow herb which grew by her arm. Jamie's passage back through the grass was plainly audible and she raised her head in time to see that he carried a bundle beneath his arm. Then he was gone, vanishing into Ladywood as if he had never been.

Slowly she got to her feet, smoothing down her dimity gown and frowning at a green grass stain which spoiled the red and white stripes. Without hesitation she descended the bank to the stable.

The pony shifted, turning his shaggy head to look at her.

"It's all right, Jinks, it's only me," she said softly, patting the dusty brown coat. She looked around the dark stall. The little dogcart stood next to bales of straw, and tackle hung from various hooks. Jinks nibbled from the manger, his large, soft eyes watching her as she moved from his side toward the ladder leading up into the small loft.

The hay had been disturbed recently, wisps hung raggedly over the edge of the loft and lay at the foot of the ladder. That was where Jamie had been. She began to climb, holding her skirts in one hand and praying the ladder was more sturdy than it looked. Then she was in the loft. On the roof she could hear the pigeons cooing together, fluttering now and then, and somewhere in the hay a mouse squeaked and rustled.

There seemed to be nothing untoward, nothing to show why Jamie had once hidden something that needed now such careful and quiet collecting. Then she saw the stitched corner of the canvas mail bag. It was partly hidden by the straw, but Jamie had been less than careful for some reason, and Jessica swept the hay aside and drew out the bag. The seals were intact and by its weight she knew nothing had been tampered with inside. A rotting rope lay by the opening down into the stable and she tied it as tightly around the bag as she could, dragging it across the hay until she could slowly lower it to the ground. Jinks shied as the bag swung close to him, but she called gently to him and he quieted, rolling his eyes warily as the bag flopped to the ground and the rope snaked down after it.

She climbed quickly down the ladder and ran to the cottage, tapping on the kitchen window and almost stopping Tamsin's heart.

"Come quickly, Tamsin, and see what I've found."

The two women looked at the mail bag.

"Well, Miss Jess, that be a proper turn-up. The mail coach were held up at Hangman's Cross about two months ago. It have happened before and since, but the mail bag was never took. This must be the one as was took that one time. But how did you find it?"

Jessica told her about Jamie Pike.

"Jamie? Well, I never. He've got a good posi-

49

tion now with Sir Francis, so what do he want to go highwaying for? He'm a proper handful—always was and always will be."

"But what shall we do? I cannot return the bag to the authorities and tell them about Jamie."

" 'Tis no more than the young hosebird deserves!"

"Yes, but he is still Jamie and I've known him all my life. The penalty for holding up the mail coach is terribly harsh."

"Ah, that it be right enough. You could always take the mail back and say as you found it in the loft here. There's no need to mention Jamie at all."

"I shall do that then. Oh, Tamsin, whatever is going on around here? There are poachers, smugglers, and now apparently, highwaymen as well. Life was almost more peaceful in London."

"Oh, Henbury were always a lively place and all," said Tamsin wryly. "Us'll take it in the dogcart in the morning. Mr. Palethorpe, the magistrate, will know what's right to do."

"But you are expecting to visit Dolly Dowdeswell. I will go. Isn't Friday the day the wagonette goes round the outlying farms to take the women to market?"

"Aye, Friday's market day."

"Then I shall halt the wagonette as it passes. If Mr. Palethorpe wants the bag, he'll have to send someone out for it."

"If you wants to go, fair enough. But, Miss Jess, there'll be plenty of folks to recognize you."

"It must be done sometime."

There was little room in the wagonette, for it

was loaded with baskets of vegetables, bundles of fagots, balls of spindle wool gleaned from hedges, and seven buxom women whose chatter ceased instantly as Jessica climbed aboard. She took the place they grudgingly moved to provide, and sat next to a woman with a large basket containing a plump red hen that clucked angrily at each lurch of the wagon. The silence was oppressive, and Jessica kept her head averted to look out at the track as it slipped away behind them.

Down the narrow track between the honeysuckle hedges and over the ford plodded the oxen, the water deep enough to reach the axles of the slow vehicle. The market was already well under way—a clutter of tables, stalls, and booths, with small flocks of sheep penned before the White Horse tavern, and some goats tethered to a rail beneath a ramshackle canvas tent. The noise was unbearable after the quiet of Applegarth and, she thought dryly, the awful hush of the wagonette. No doubt the whole of Henbury would soon know that the notorious Miss Durleigh was in the town.

Her business with Mr. Palethorpe was quickly accomplished and he promised that an officer would come soon to collect the mail bag. It would be some hours before the wagonette began its homeward journey, and so she wandered slowly around the town, seeking out remembered places and now and then seeing people who had once been her friends. But each and every one turned their faces away from her, and she heard one or two unkind remarks that she knew she was fully meant to hear. She paused by the lych-gate into

51

St. Mary's churchyard. The Woodville family tomb lay ahead, beneath a spreading yew tree, and her heart tightened as she saw the grave with its fresh flowers and still-raised earth. Philip, the man she had given up everything for and whom she had loved so much, lay there, cold and remote beneath the damp earth. So near, and yet so infinitely far away. Tears pricked her eyes and she opened her reticule to take out a handkerchief. She was about to hurry away when a figure caught her eye.

A little old woman with a straight back, her face hidden by the veil of her hat, sat upright on the bench beneath the yew tree, her gloved hands resting like claws on the pearl handle of her cane. Lady Amelia Woodville was staring at her younger son's grave without moving. Nearby, a maid waited patiently. Jessica watched for a moment, feeling oddly cold at seeing that quiet, calm vigil. She turned away at last, her slippers tapping on the cobbles as she retraced her steps towards the center of the town.

She found herself by the apothecary's shop, staring in at the array of bottles, packets, and boxes that lined the dark, narrow shelves inside. Polished brass handles on the many tiny drawers gleamed in the dull interior, and she could see the slow swing of the pendulum clock on the wall behind the counter.

A large coach rattled along the street, stopping at Miss Brendon's haberdashery opposite, and Jessica turned quickly to see Rosamund climb down, telling the coachman to go to the church to find Lady Amelia.

Rosamund stood for a moment before the bow

windows of the shop, looking at the array of ribbons and laces displayed there. Jessica stared at her, for she had forgotten how graceful and beautiful Rosamund was with her pale golden hair, fine complexion, and elegant figure. She was dressed in a turquoise pelisse and straw bonnet with bright blue ribbons that fluttered as she pushed open the door. The jingle of the bell carried across the road over the noise of an oxcart that lumbered slowly by.

On impulse, Jessica crossed the street to look in the window past the rainbow of colorful ribbons to where Rosamund stood at the counter discussing a bolt of fabric with the fussy Miss Brendon. Rosamund was shaking her head and Miss Brendon held up her finger and then hurried into the storeroom.

Almost before it was thought of Jessica had opened the door and entered the shop. "Rosamund?"

Rosamund's eyes darkened. "I don't wish to speak with you."

"I know. I know that. But I just wanted to tell you that I am sorry."

"Sorry that you stole my husband?"

"I loved him."

"And I did not, therefore it was in order to take him?"

"Please, Rosamund, I do not wish to remain at odds with you."

"Then stay away from me."

Anger stirred her and Jessica felt provoked into retaliating. "Your attitude is somewhat unbelievable, Rosamund, when you look down your nose at me. Your widowhood is recent and yet you do not wear black. Do not cast stones at me for my conduct when your own does not bear close scrutiny."

Rosamund stepped back, her hand clenching the bolt of fabric on the counter, but then she gained control. "Such a low outburst is what I would expect of you, Jessica." She turned her back and the conversation, painful and disastrous as it had been, was at an end.

Jessica closed her eyes faintly. Why had she attacked Rosamund like that? Why? Now the barrier was, if anything, greater than before. Slowly she turned and walked from the shop.

She found herself back at the market square, although she was not too aware of how she had got there. Tears blurred her eyes and she bowed her head so no one should see her face. The wagonette had another two hours to wait. But two hours were unendurable in the circumstances, and she walked around the edge of the market and back on the road towards Varangian and Applegarth. Outside the Feathers she paused. The ford was too deep to cross on foot and men were repairing the rickety footbridge that had been in need of attention for some time.

Miserably she hesitated on the edge of the stream, watching the green weed swaying as the current rushed past. Rosamund's words still rung in her ears, and she was struggling with her tears and did not hear the horseman rein in behind her.

"Do you wish to cross over, Miss Durleigh?"

Sir Nicholas leaned forward on the pommel to look at her. He wore a blue riding jacket and buff, high-waisted breeches, and his dark, curly hair caught the breeze as he doffed his hat.

"I do, Sir Nicholas," she answered, hoping that her bonnet afforded sufficient shadow to hide her tears.

"If you can stomach so odious a prospect, I would be delighted to carry you across."

"I accept your offer, sir," she whispered in a small voice.

He dismounted and lifted her onto the saddle, mounting again behind her. She sat sideways, looking down at the water as the horse moved easily across the ford. Her arms were tight around his waist as the animal struggled up the sharp incline at the other side and then moved up the lane between the high hedges.

"You are going back to Applegarth, Miss Durleigh?"

"Yes."

"Then allow me to take you all the way for I, unfortunately, have business at Varangian."

"Unfortunately?" She looked up quickly.

He smiled. "It is so very far when one has other things one wishes to do first," he said by way of explanation. But she was left with the impression that he had chosen the word for another reason.

They rode in silence, and he made no comment upon the loud sniffs he heard occasionally, nor did he seem to notice the number of times she took her handkerchief from her reticule.

As they reached Applegarth he reined in to dismount. She stretched down to him and he could no longer pretend that he did not know she was crying.

"Was Henbury so very unkind then?"

"I spoke with Rosamund."

He set her gently on the ground. "A grave mistake, I would imagine."

"Yes."

"And you chose an unfortunate day, for she had already been set about the ears by my mother who is outraged at her sudden setting aside of widow's weeds in favor of more happy garb. Lady Amelia is something of a stickler for the proprieties, I fear."

Jessica heard this with a sinking heart.

"But, Miss Durleigh, let me speak of something more pleasing to your ears. The audit revealed nothing untoward concerning Philip."

"I did not think that it would."

"You alone would appear to have such faith in him. I almost envy him for being loved so completely and so faithfully. And I never cease to marvel at how blind that emotion can be."

"You are all wrong about him," she said stoutly, conquering the urge to sniff again.

"Among the army of marching men you alone are in step? Come now, Miss Durleigh, that is hardly likely to be so."

"I believe that I am right, Sir Nicholas, and I will stand by the man *I* knew."

He remounted. "That is fair enough, for everyone should speak as they find. I salute your loyalty, madam." He doffed his hat again, and then turned the horse toward Varangian and rode up the incline.

She watched him for a moment and then straightened her bonnet, taking a deep breath. She was glad Tamsin would be with Dolly Dowdewsell still, for she could attend to her face without any further uncomfortable questions. The matter of the visit to Henbury was something Jessica wished to forget.

swell, etc., for she could afford to buy this
without any further comprehensible question. The
matter of his gain in disobey was confusing
whence whatever he had.

Chapter 7

Two weeks later the invitation to the ball at Varangian was delivered at Applegarth. Jessica put the gold-edged card beside the pile of beans on the table and Tamsin looked at her.

"Shall you be going then?"

"I don't think so."

Tamsin looked at it, reading slowly. " 'Please come, Jessica, for I think it would be the best course, both for Henbury and for you. Francis.' Well, happen Sir Francis do think you should."

"I couldn't." The recent disaster of her visit to Henbury was too strong and painful.

"Listen, Miss Jess, 'tis time the folks hereabouts realized you'm not one of them 'ladies' entertaining different men each night, and sometimes in the day as well! You made a mistake—and mistake it were, so don't go pretending it weren't—and now 'tis all done with. A start has to be made somewhere and this ball do seem as good a spot as any."

"I could not endure so embarrassing an evening, Tamsin. Truly, I couldn't. They would all stare and whisper, and only the most lecherous of the men would offer to partner me. It would all be too much. And Rosamund would be there."

"You always could handle that one. Ignore her, Miss Jess. Pretend she don't exist. Balls is for enjoyment, for prettying yourself up and having a good time. You think on it a little. Old Tamsin knows what's best for you, and skulking here all the time ain't right at all."

"I will think about it, but I don't really want to go. Francis means well, but it wouldn't be right for me to foist myself on Henbury society when that society most plainly does not want me."

Tamsin went on slicing the beans, glancing out of the window. "Someone's paying a visit. I wonder who he be?"

A man with a thin, nervous face rode a stout gray cob across the orchard toward the cottage. He was dressed in a brown cloth coat of a good cut without being too fashionable, and as he dismounted he wiped his forehead with his kerchief, as if unsettled, or even shocked. Jessica opened the door to him, rather alarmed at the pallor of his face.

"Er, Miss Durleigh? Miss Jessica Durleigh?"

"I am, sir. Please come in. Are you all right?" She drew a chair quickly and motioned him to sit down.

"Thank you kindly, madam. I fear I have had something of a fright. I was just leaving the

Feathers when there was a commotion outside. It appears some mail from a lost mail bag was at last being handed out to the various people whose letters had gone astray, and Sir Francis Varangian was passing. There was a letter for him. He took one look at it, went as white as a sheet and drove his curricle blindly forward without looking. He almost drove over me. I am not a fine rider at the best of times, and it gave me such a fright. Dear me, I have never seen Sir Francis in such a way before. He did not halt to apologize, nor even say anything. He just drove on over the ford and away. So unlike him—oh, dear me, yes. Now then, Miss Durleigh, allow me to introduce myself. I am Jethro Slade, the jeweler of Bath. My card."

She took the little card. "Mr. Slade?" Why had he come to see her?

"I was beginning to be concerned as to what I should do, and then the letter arrived yesterday and set my mind at rest."

"I am afraid, sir, that I do not understand."

"The necklace Mr. Philip Woodville commissioned."

Slade's of Bath. Suddenly she remembered the receipt Nicholas had shown her. "But Mr. Philip is. . . ."

"Oh, I realize he cannot be here, for indeed the letter came from London only yesterday."

Her face was still. "Is this some joke, Mr. Slade?"

"Joke? Oh, dear me, I hope not. I have the letter here. It is Mr. Philip's writing, is it not?" He took a creased envelope from his waistcoat pocket and handed it to her.

"Yes, yes, it is his writing." Her hands shook a little and she gave it back quickly. "But, Mr. Slade,

61

the letter cannot have come only yesterday, for Philip has been dead for some months now." How terribly cold and detached the words sounded. Suddenly she thought of the stolen mail bag. "Could it perhaps have been in the mail bag which was stolen at Hangman's Cross?"

The jeweler was blinking as he absorbed the news of Philip's death. "Dead you say? Oh, dear me, dear, dear me. Stolen mail bag? Yes, I suppose that it could. Sometimes my mail is re-routed this way. It is possible. Oh, my dear Miss Durleigh, I trust that I have not caused you any distress by my visit, but truly I did not know."

"Of course you did not, Mr. Slade. Please do not concern yourself so."

He polished his glasses busily on a cloth, looking shortsightedly at her. "I had had the necklace for so long that I had begun to worry over it—it is so valuable, don't you see. Most definitely the finest piece I have ever created—from the finest stones, of course, but nonetheless I am very proud of it. The letter told me to deliver the necklace to Miss Durleigh at Applegarth, and so here it is." He took a long, red leather box from his pocket and laid it in her hands.

She opened the box and saw the necklace resting on its cushion of black velvet. It was so magnificent that she caught her breath, and Tamsin set down her vegetable knife with a clatter as she, too, stared at the flashing, brilliant beauty of the diamonds. They were large and clear and perfectly matched, and an exquisite adornment for any woman's throat; but all Jessica could think of was the enormous price Philip had paid for it.

Mr. Slade cleared his throat. "I must confess to

being somewhat relieved at having discharged my duty in this. I confess also that such a necklace deserves so beautiful an owner."

"It is mine?"

"Oh, yes. It was commissioned simply and solely for you. Mr. Philip was quite adamant, and the letter was confirmation of that. I shall be proud indeed when next you attend a ball and my creation draws the admiration of one and all."

A ball. Jessica looked quickly at Tamsin. Was this perhaps a sign that she should go to Varangian after all?

"Mr. Slade, do you know the nearest posting inn?"

"Why, yes. The Feathers is one such now, for there are postboys in their yellow jackets, and this afternoon I saw a post-chaise in the yard."

Jessica came to a sudden decision. "Then, Tamsin, I shall go after all." She lifted the necklace from its box. "Can you imagine anything finer to set off the yellow silk evening gown?"

"No, Miss Jess, nothing finer on earth. And now, Mr. Slade, shall you take a glass of Madeira before you return?"

"Why thank you, thank you kindly. I am still a little unnerved by my encounter with Sir Francis."

Tamsin smoothed her apron and brought some sparkling glasses from a cupboard. The amber-colored wine made a pleasing sound as it was poured, and the jeweler watched appreciatively. "There are few finer wines, Miss Durleigh. I've always had a taste for good Madeira."

He drank, almost smacking his lips with pleasure. Tamsin's nose twitched; the jeweler tried to act like gentry, when he was no better than she was.

The Madeira, however, proved stronger than the unfortunate Mr. Slade had imagined, for after the second glass he was smiling genially, his cheeks red and his eyes bright. He stood to take his leave, reaching unsteadily for his hat, and his glance fell upon the necklace's box. "Strange thing that, it's been puzzling me. I always thought they couldn't stand the sight of each other."

"Who?" Jessica handed him the hat.

"Mr. Woodville and Sir Francis."

"Why do you say that?"

He patted the hat on his head. "The necklace. Paid for by Mr. Woodville with a draft from Sir Francis." His smile faded uncomfortably. "Upon my word, Miss Durleigh, again I must ask your forgiveness. My last comments were indiscreet and not at all what should have been said. Don't know what came over me."

"You say that Sir Francis put up the money for the necklace?"

He cleared his throat. "Not exactly. The money came originally from Varangian—more than that I cannot say. See, it is here in my little book." He fished a small leather book from his pocket and flipped the pages until he came to the one he sought. "There."

She took it and saw the neat writing. There was no mistake—Philip had indeed paid with money from Francis. But why? Why on earth would Francis have dealings with Philip whom he neither liked nor respected? And why so vast a sum for such a purpose? She closed the book thoughtfully.

The newly raddled floor was slippery, and Mr. Slade's equilibrium most certainly suspect now. He took a step toward the door and his boot slid alarmingly. Tamsin squeaked as she reached out to steady him, and Jessica forgot the book as she accompanied the jeweler to his patient cob.

He had left Applegarth on his return journey when she realized that she still had the book. Neither she nor Tamsin spoke in the quiet kitchen where the only sound was the steady slicing of the beans. A sense of unease pervaded Jessica as she looked at the book and the necklace. How much was there that she did not know? She locked them both in a cupboard and put the key in her reticule. "Tamsin?" She turned to look at the older woman.

"I don't know, Miss Jess, I just don't know. And that's a fact."

Chapter 8

"How do I look, Tamsin?"

Jessica surveyed her reflection in the long mirror. The high-waisted, sheer, yellow silk gown clung revealingly and she bit her lip. Was it perhaps a little too daring for Henbury society? But Philip had so liked her in it; the yellow, he had said, had set off her chestnut hair to perfection.

"Well, Miss Jess, I don't rightly know."

"I shall change it then."

"No, no, don't take on so. I was thinking that perhaps a little less blanch and a little more of that there Portuguese rouge or whatever it be called. Right now you looks a little as if you'm ill."

"It's the fashion. One must look pale and fragile."

"Well you looks *that* all right, and no mistake. But it do seem a pity, toning down your pretty coloring merely to follow a fashion."

"And did you never follow fashion, Tamsin? Not even in your giddy youth?"

"My youth weren't giddy. But happen you're right, I didn't feel as how I were dressed lessen I had the latest falderal, whether it suited me or no."

"What about my hair then?"

"Well, 'tis short and wavy and it do shine a treat."

"Yes, but what ornaments shall I dress it with?"

"The gold band with the low-curling ostrich feather, that were the one I liked best."

"I agree." Jessica picked it up from the dressing table and set it carefully over her curls, tweaking them into place around the simple gold fillet. The fluffy ostrich feather curled in exactly the right way to draw attention to the diamond necklace. How the stones flashed and twinkled in the evening sun streaming through the window. She drew on the fine white evening gloves, stretching her fingers until all was comfortable, then she put on the dress rings she had earlier decided upon. "Now, Tamsin, what else is there?"

"The fan, your reticule, your slippers and the mantle."

A moment later they heard the crunch of wheels and the stamping of horses outside. Then someone knocked smartly at the door.

"Tamsin. The chaise is here already and I'm not ready!"

"Don't get in a tizzy now, for he'll not go without you, 'specially as he wants his ten shillings yet." Tamsin slipped the red-lined evening mantle over Jessica's shoulders and tied its ribbons carefully.

Jessica lowered her eyes. "I have not worn this since Philip took me to Drury Lane last spring, just before...."

"Don't think of such things now, for you're going to enjoy yourself."

"I still wonder if I am doing the right thing. They won't like it."

"Then they can go and do the other thing then, can't they? *All* of 'em!"

The postboy's yellow jacket was spotless and the yellow post-chaise was polished until it gleamed. The innkeeper of the Feathers had turned the vehicle out smartly, no doubt knowing that it would be a fine advertisement at so important a function as the summer ball at Varangian Hall. She sat back on the brown velvet upholstered seats, swallowing as the postboy shut the door with a loud bang. This was a foolish notion; she should be paying more attention to her instinct that was telling her to get out and return to the safety of Applegarth. But already the team was drawing the chaise in a large semicircle over the orchard, and she just had time to lean out to wave to Tamsin before it gathered speed to climb the incline behind the cottage.

A dog barked at the noise and she looked out to catch a glimpse of Jamie Pike walking along a path that led into Ladywood, turning to call Nipper who was capering around the wheels of the chaise. After a final demonstration of his ferocity, Nipper turned obediently to pad after his master. Jessica saw Jamie vault lightly over a stile in the fence bounding the wood.

The long driveway leading across the park of Varangian Hall was lit by colored lanterns in the trees, and on the lake the boats carried torches that flickered brightly, sending reflections dancing on the water. Closer to the Hall sparkling lights illuminated the fountains and statues, and the tall windows of the house were ablaze. Strains of music drifted on the warm air as the chaise joined the throng of coaches and gigs forming a crush before the house.

Jessica clasped her hands nervously in her lap, glancing to the side of the great house where she could see people walking in the orangery. She smiled, for Francis had been so proud of the orange trees, and even in the half-light of evening she could see the fruit hanging heavily on the green branches. A footman was lighting Chinese lanterns that were laced among them, and another was spraying a fine mist of water over the blossoms. Even so important an event as the summer ball must not interfere with the care of the precious oranges.

She turned her attention to the other window of the chaise, and to her surprise found herself looking into Nicholas Woodville's startled face. The Woodville barouche had drawn alongside, and a quick glance told her that he was accompanied by Rosamund who, as yet, had not seen her. Nicholas inclined his head coolly and then looked away. His profile stirred her memories painfully, for he *was* so like Philip. A little older

70

and sterner, yes, but still it was Philip she could see echoed in the fine lips and dark eyes.

Rosamund was looking up at Varangian, her eyes shining. Was she perhaps thinking of Francis, wondered Jessica, sitting back farther into the shadows of the chaise. Rosamund's pale golden hair was hidden beneath a green silk turban that was hung with pearls, and thick strands of pearls glowed at her throat where her mantle was loose. She had an almost ethereal beauty, decided Jessica enviously, and could so easily have been the toast of London had Philip so desired.

The door of the chaise opened suddenly and the postboy leaned in. "Begging your pardon, miss, but you had best get out here and walk the last few steps. There's a landau up by the steps with a broken axle and I doubt if you'll reach the steps in under an hour if you wait here." He turned to look at the clock over the stables and cleared his throat a little.

She followed his glance. "You have another customer to attend to," she accused.

His eyes wavered away from her face. "Only a small fare, miss. Just from Henbury out to Beckitt's End. I'll be back well in time to return you to Applegarth."

"You had better be or there will be no ten shillings for the Feathers!"

"I'll be back, miss. I swear I will."

Angrily she climbed down. "I shall have something to say about this, and you may tell the landlord as much. Ten shillings is for the hire of the chaise for an entire evening, not merely to accomplish the journey either way."

71

"Yes, miss." The postboy touched his cap respectfully, but then was up on the seat with the reins in his hands. Jessica moved swiftly away from the chaise, for she did not want to be seen from the Woodville barouche. She had reached the steps when at last the postboy managed to maneuver the chaise out of the long line of vehicles by turning it across the smooth green lawn where the wheels left ruts and the horses' hooves kicked up clods of earth. She heard a footman shouting angrily and waving his fist, but the chaise did not stop, it merely increased its speed until it was swaying dangerously toward the wrought iron gates, out of sight at the end of the avenue of trees.

Fresh laurel leaves and flowers had been strewn like a meadow over the wide steps, and a little Negro boy dressed in blue satin bowed sweepingly at each guest entering the circular entrance hall with its black and white tiles and marble statues. As a maid took her mantle, Jessica looked up at the magnificent ceiling painted to resemble a scene from Greek mythology. She smoothed her gown and pulled on her gloves more tightly. The very size of Varangian she had somehow not remembered. She felt almost lost in that immense vestibule where at least twelve liveried footmen stood lining the way to the ballroom and where maids received the mantles and cloaks of each new arrival. She had so nearly been mistress of all this. She walked up the red-carpeted steps to the gold and white doors of the ballroom. This was the worst moment now, the moment when everyone would realize that she was a guest here. The notorious Miss Jessica Durleigh, the fallen woman who had so brazenly lived with another woman's husband and had had the nerve to return to the town she had so scandalized. Taking a deep breath, she gave her name to the master of ceremonies.

Chapter 9

"Miss Jessica Durleigh."

The name rang out over the ballroom as if accompanied by a thunderclap. Immediately every head turned toward the head of the stairs. Almost, thought Jessica, as if drawn by invisible strings.

Francis turned from his conversation with Mr. Palethorpe, the magistrate, and walked slowly up the steps to greet her. She was shocked by the way Francis had changed. His good-natured face was cold and he did not smile as he bowed over her hand.

"Francis?"

He said nothing, but took her hand to lead her down the steps. He looked splendid in a black velvet evening coat, and the silver threads of his high waistcoat were shining and costly. A large and complicated cravat bloomed at his throat, and she was surprised at the extreme height of his modish collar. "Miss Durleigh, I trust that you will enjoy yourself, although I fear that Somerset cannot offer the pleasures and delights of London."

She inclined her head slowly, noticing how swiftly he dropped her hand. He was so cold and distant, and so very unlike the Francis she had spoken to last that she could only stand alone watching him as he went to greet the next guest.

Curious glances were thrown in her direction and she was conscious of the whispers spreading through the crowded ballroom as she took a glass of punch from the tray held out by a footman. She moved away from the conspicuous area by the tables and went toward a more shadowy area by a decorated pillar. Green leaves and flowers had been carefully twined around the columns in sweet-smelling garlands, with spicy pomanders regularly spaced between. The chandeliers glittered brightly, reflected in the mirrors that lined the walls of the gold and white room. At the far end a fashionable Bath orchestra played a mazurka.

An interested buzz rippled through the crowd as the master of ceremonies struck the floor with his staff to announce Nicholas and Rosamund.

Again the string pulled and all eyes swiveled toward Jessica and then to Rosamund, a vision in gold and green striped silk that shimmered as she descended the steps on Nicholas' arm. Then it happened. She happened to look across the ballroom straight at Jessica. Her steps faltered and she stopped, her fingers digging into Nicholas' arm so that he turned in surprise. Rosamund stared at Jessica, her face suddenly pale and angry, and without a word she turned around and left the ballroom. Nicholas stood alone, undecided whether to go after her or to continue down the steps. After barely a moment he decided that Rosamund must do as she pleased, for he continued the descent to where a startled Francis waited for him. The moment hung, then the orchestra struck up a cotillion and the concentrated attention of the gathering was distracted.

Jessica closed her eyes weakly. How ever had she been fool enough to come here? It was grossly unfair of her to inflict herself upon Rosamund, and now it was obvious that Francis had thought better of his earlier kindness. She watched Nicholas bowing to Francis, noticing how refined and tasteful he looked in a coat of dark brown velvet and cream trousers that looked straight from Old Bond Street. His hair was fashionably curled around his face, and a discreet cravat burgeoned at his throat. Lace spilled from his cuffs as he sketched another bow and left Francis.

Her heart sank, for it was immediately obvious that he was coming to speak with her. There was nothing she could do but stand by the column and wait for him.

"Miss Durleigh."

"Sir Nicholas."

"Perhaps I should have told Rosamund about your being here *before* she entered Varangian, for then she would have turned away without making so damnable a scene."

She colored. "She is within her rights to act as she did."

"No one is within any rights to behave so tactlessly, Miss Durleigh. Surely the fashionable drawing rooms of London taught you that."

"The fashionable drawing rooms of London were not open to such as I, Sir Nicholas, as you very well know."

He smiled thinly. "I see no reason why not, for they open their doors to those who conduct their private lives in far more disreputable a manner than you. At least you were honest and open about your *affaire de coeur*."

"To be honest was the mistake, Sir Nicholas. Had I married Francis and then commenced an affair with Philip, then, no doubt, all would have been well. But that is a reflection of our times, is it not?" She looked at him without smiling. If he wished to speak of such things, then she would give as good as she got.

"Do not descend to my level, Miss Durleigh, for I swear it does not suit you."

"Please leave me alone, sir, for I would rather endure the atmosphere of this place than your company."

His eyes suddenly went to the diamond necklace. "I mark the style of the excellent Mr. Slade," he murmured, looking at her once more.

She felt the need to defend herself. "I knew nothing of the necklace when you asked me."

"I did not for one moment think otherwise, madam. Come, let us set our dueling aside and enjoy a glass of champagne together. Please." He took her hand suddenly. "Please, for I wish to make amends for my lamentable behavior hitherto. Besides, it would seem to me that we are both here against our will."

"You? However would *you* be forced into coming if you wished not to?"

"Oh, let us say I wished to please Rosamund."

"Let us say you are being untruthful, for you would not do anything merely to please any woman, Sir Nicholas. Fashionable London society taught me that much about members of the strong sex. You have another reason—one you obviously would prefer not to mention."

"And you are too penetrating by far, Miss Durleigh, which amazes me when I consider how my late brother gulled you so completely."

"Have you already forgotten your resolution to be more agreeable?"

He smiled. "But you must be beginning to wonder about Philip." He dragged his forefinger over the diamonds at her throat. "You are no fool, Jessica."

"I wonder only why everyone disliked him so, for I saw only good in him. I loved him dearly, and ever will."

"I pray you will not shed tears right now, Miss Durleigh, for I would find it uncommon disturbing, especially in front of so many inquisitive eyes."

"I shall not embarrass you, Sir Nicholas."

"I thank heaven for it. Now, some champagne?" He did not wait for a reply but snapped his fingers at a footman who in a moment brought a bottle and two glasses which he sat on a small pedestal table close by.

She sipped it, watching him as he replaced the bottle on the table. "Miss Durleigh, about our . . . er, encounter . . . in Ladywood."

"Encounter? Sir Nicholas, I cannot think what you mean."

He smiled. "I thank you, madam, for I would greatly dislike my activities to become common knowledge."

"What were you doing?"

"One day perhaps I shall tell you, but for now—a toast. To the coming year of 1818, may it prove more gentle than its predecessor."

"To 1818."

"Yes, and I trust it will bring a inkling of sanity to Rosamund."

"In what way?"

"She is infatuated with Varangian."

"And why should that be termed 'insanity'? Philip gave her nothing; she has no reason to mourn his passing. Francis is a good man, kind and. . . ."

"Spare me the man's undoubted virtues."

"Why so contemptuous? You don't like Francis?"

"One must *like* him?"

"One must like someone in this world, Sir Nicholas, and I fast come to the conclusion that you neither like nor respect anyone at all."

"On the contrary, madam, for against all my better judgment I both like and respect *you*." He raised his glass to her.

"You mock me I think, sir."

"No, Miss Durleigh, I am perfectly serious."

Embarrassed by the expression in his eyes, she looked away past him to the unsteady figure of Mr. Palethorpe. The old-fashioned magistrate was quickly seizing a full glass from a passing tray before wending his way toward Nicholas.

Nicholas turned as the magistrate tweaked his arm. "My dear Palethorpe, you *do* appear to have enjoyed your evening thus far." He rescued the brimming glass from the wobbling hand.

" 'Pon my soul, yes. Been waiting since this time last year." He dug Nicholas in the ribs and laughed uproariously. "D'you know, Woodville, I've tasted the finest cognac I've ever sampled in my life. Here, here in Varangian. Would that my merchant stocked the same."

"Your merchant, no doubt, does not creep through Ladywood with a train of donkeys, Palethorpe."

"Eh?" The magistrate straightened his periwig, only managing to make his squiffy appearance all the worse. "Donkeys d'you say? Oh! Oh, yes, *donkeys*. Oh, well, that explains it, of course."

"Being magistrate, I fear, excludes you from the fraternity enjoying the spoils of smuggling."

"I'd close me eyes for the sake of a bottle or so, Woodville," he said wistfully.

Nicholas smiled. "I see that the Widow Claybone is smiling and nodding at you so, I fear her head will shake loose from her neck. Pray go and make her evening complete."

Mr. Palethorpe glanced surreptitiously at the lady in question. "Can't stand crimson taffeta, d'you know; a thoroughly disreputable fabric if ever I saw one." He took a deep breath and snatched his glass from Nicholas, draining it in one gulp, then straightening his periwig again. "An uncommon handsome woman though, eh, Woodville?"

"Uncommon indeed."

The magistrate glanced down at his buckled shoes and carefully wiped one clean against his white hose before walking in a reasonably straight manner toward the widow Claybone who was all blushes and dimples as she curtsied to him.

Jessica's attention was drawn back to Nicholas. "This is rumored to be a dance, Miss Durleigh, and yet we have not taken to the floor."

"Nor have I any wish to. I feel sufficiently conspicuous already. Tell me, Sir Nicholas, is anything wrong here at Varangian?"

"Wrong? In what way?"

"Francis seems—well, upset." She watched Francis as he partnered a pretty dark girl in lemon muslin.

"Something in that wayward mail bag would appear to have disturbed his equilibrium, or so Rosamund informs me. I, too, had remarked his pallor and uncertain temper." He held out his arm. "This dance, Miss Durleigh?"

She shook her head. "No, Sir Nicholas, I thank you, but I am too fainthearted. Surely there are many excited female hearts fluttering at the thought of a measure with you."

He inclined his head. "I am sure you would never be fainthearted, Miss Durleigh, so please do not shatter my new illusions by saying such regrettable things about yourself." He raised her hand to his lips and then was gone, mingling with the crowd on the floor until she could no longer make him out.

She jumped as a footman bowed before her. "Miss Durleigh? Sir Francis begs to speak with you in private. If you will accompany me to the study."

Unaccountably her heart fell, for Francis' earlier behavior on greeting her did not bode well for any interview. She nodded to the footman and followed him from the ballroom.

Chapter 10

The long portrait gallery was quiet after the noise of the ballroom, although strains of music still echoed along the carpeted rooms and corridors as Jessica followed the footman toward Francis' private apartments.

He stood by the fireplace gazing at the dark red wine in his glass, swirling it occasionally. He looked up and she saw that his face was still chill. He glanced at the footman. "The keepers are out?"

"Yes, Sir Francis, they have been out some two hours now."

"If any poachers are sighted I am to be notified immediately. No summer ball will keep me occupied while they poach my game."

"Yes, Sir Francis." The footman bowed and closed the double doors behind him.

Francis crossed the room to a sideboard where he poured himself a second glass of wine, and she could not help but notice that he did not offer her any refreshment. "Well, Jessica, you gulled me completely and no mistake. It seems my lot in life to be made a fool of by you."

"What do you mean?" She stared, taken aback.

"Do not act the innocent now, for we are alone and may speak freely."

"I do not know what you are talking about, and I most certainly do not like your tone."

"Indeed? Then what tone should I employ when addressing you? One of humility? Of reverence, perhaps? Maybe even begging? You truly are a wonderful actress, Jessica, for I could almost believe the look of innocent incomprehension on your exquisite face."

"What has happened, Francis? Why are you saying these terrible things to me?"

"I thought it was just Philip, that it could only be him. I did not for one moment believe that you could have been involved, too. When he died, I actually thought that *that* was at last the end of it. But no. It has begun again and there is only you now to be the instigator."

She walked toward the door. "I think you must be in your cups, sir, and so will not remain in your company one moment longer."

He smiled, but his eyes remained cold. "It is not a pleasant sensation to feel threatened, is it? You and Philip between you have played me like a salmon on a line these past two years, but I am not to be hooked anymore. You may like to digest that fact for a moment."

"For heaven's sake, Francis, I do not know what you are talking about. Believe me."

"This is what I am talking about!" He flung an envelope on the desk beside him. "This filthy demand which has been bleeding me since. . . ." He broke off and waved his arm helplessly.

"May I see it?"

"*See* it? Why? You of all people must know what it contains."

"But I don't. I have never seen it before and I know nothing of what it contains."

She seemed so utterly at a loss that he doubted his suspicions for the first time. "Sweet Lord, Jessica, I could willingly believe you, but I cannot. I dare not. If it was only Philip—and I know it was he for he told me so, he even laughed about it—why has this arrived now, so long after his death? You *must* have sent it."

"The mail bag that was stolen. Just as Mr. Slade the jeweler received a letter from Philip only recently, so also have you received one."

"The mail bag was recovered from *Applegarth!*"

"With the seal unbroken. How dare you hint that I was in any way guilty of tampering with the King's Mail!"

"Jess, this is a matter of life and death to me now. I can no longer stand the leeching."

"I believe that whatever it is is important, for truly, sir, you act in a most irrational way."

"Blackmail is what we talk of, Jess. How else do you imagine your precious Philip could have provided you with trinkets like that necklace?"

She flinched. "I do not believe you. Philip would

87

never have stooped to such a thing." But she felt suddenly cold inside.

"Philip Woodville was a first class louse, a bloodsucking heap of filth whose every breath was a sin against mankind." He spoke reasonably, as if commenting upon the weather.

Her eyes were huge. "I will not hear you say those things about him. I *will* not!"

"The time has come now for the truth to be admitted, Jess. It is the end of the tunnel and I see daylight ahead. I'll not pay a penny. Do your worst."

"Oh, Francis, Francis, you are so wrong about everything."

"Read it then. Go on, read it, for its meaning is plain enough, and the writing is Philip's."

She took the letter from the envelope. The words were simple, and as Francis had said, their meaning was unmistakable. Francis was to deliver the sum of two thousand guineas to the writer immediately, or know the consequences. She closed her eyes, her mouth running dry suddenly. "It could be that you owed him the sum," she whispered.

In answer he took a bundle of similar letters from a drawer, tossing them at her feet. "Each month I received one such, sometimes for less money, sometimes for infinitely more. Do you still deny the truth?"

Miserably she looked at him, carefully folding the letter and replacing it in its envelope. She jumped as an urgent knock sounded on the door behind her. The footman spoke quickly. "It's the poachers, Sir Francis. The keepers have sent a lad with the word."

"This time I'll get them. Have my horse saddled immediately."

"Yes, Sir Francis."

Francis gathered the letters and replaced them in the drawer which he then carefully locked. "Perhaps you truly are as shocked as would seem from your pallor, madam, or perhaps you still ape Mrs. Siddons. I know not. The consequences of this latest letter are unavoidable, however. I shall tell the world what has been done to me, and to hell with the result. I am, as they say, at the end of my tether." He strode past her and she turned to watch him pass along the gallery.

Slowly she left the study, her slippers making no sound on the thick carpets. Francis' ancestors stared down at her and she felt as if they, too, were accusing her. Her steps quickened as she hurried down the wide, curving staircase into the hall. The little Negro boy got to his feet from his seat on the bottom step, but she hardly saw him as she went to the main entrance. A footman bowed and she glanced at him.

"Has a post-chaise returned?"

"No, madam, there has definitely been no chaise."

Then she must stay. She turned back into the house.

"Is something wrong, Miss Durleigh?"

"No, Sir Nicholas." She turned to look at him, her eyes unnaturally bright.

"Forgive me, but I am assured by looking at you that there is indeed something wrong. Even to my unobservant male eye it would seem clear

89

that you are upset and close to tears." He took her hand and led her toward a chaise longue. "Do you wish to leave?" he asked quietly.

She nodded, her eyes still bright with unshed tears. "My chaise has not returned."

"Rosamund had the wit to send my barouche back for me. It is, of course, entirely at your disposal."

"Why are you kind to me, Sir Nicholas?"

"Why should I not be?"

"Any number of salient reasons spring to mind, sir."

"You will persist in viewing me as some ogre, Miss Durleigh, when I am not. I have not approved of your conduct in the past, but my late brother was as plausible a rogue as ever lived, and he most certainly had a way with the ladies. I believe you loved him, and that he loved you. That does not excuse your behavior, but I am content that the emotion was genuine. And should a single fall from grace, albeit a somewhat prolonged one, blacken your name forevermore?"

She clung to his hand suddenly. "May I go home now, please?" she whispered.

He snapped his fingers at the Negro boy. "The Woodville barouche, boy, and quick about it," he said, flicking a coin into the outstretched hands.

"Yes, sir!"

"Miss Durleigh, I much preferred you when you acted with defiance and spirit." Nicholas took her chin in his hand and made her look at him. "What has happened to so set you down?"

"I cannot tell you, Sir Nicholas." She looked away quickly for he was so like Philip.

The boy was there again. "The barouche, sir."

She walked with Nicholas to the doorway. Outside the night was clear and moonless and stars glittered in the dark sky. The barouche waited at the foot of the flower-strewn steps and Nicholas began to descend with her. At that moment a large party of horsemen appeared from the stables. Francis led them, urging his horse swiftly across the parkland toward the hill where Ladywood's dark outline could be seen.

Nicholas paused. "What is going on?"

"Francis and his gamekeepers are in pursuit of poachers."

"Poachers, eh? In Ladywood?"

"Yes." She looked at him. He was suddenly tense.

"Well, Miss Durleigh, I am about to foist my company upon you, I fear." He handed her swiftly into the carriage, turning to speak urgently to the coachman. "Get a move on then, Parr, and keep your eyes and ears peeled."

"Yes, Sir Nicholas." The coachman cracked his whip and the horses leapt forward, the wheels of the barouche crunching on the gravel.

Chapter 11

"*Over there, Sir Nicholas,* beneath the beech tree." Parr pointed with the whip as the barouche rattled to a standstill.

Nicholas leaned out of the window. The horses were tethered to the fence by the stile where earlier Jessica had seen Jamie Pike and Nipper. "Can you get the barouche off the road and out of sight?"

"Yes, sir." The reins slapped slightly and the barouche moved quietly off the road to a grassy verge behind an elderberry bush.

Parr climbed down, testing the brake against the rear wheels and then coming to the door. "Perhaps we'll be lucky tonight."

Nicholas nodded. "I sincerely trust so, for this has gone on long enough."

Jessica listened in surprise. There seemed some

sort of understanding between the two men, an understanding that crossed the barrier of class. Just what was Nicholas Woodville's interest in what went on in Ladywood? Was he hare, or hound?

The coachman pointed through the stile down a long gully thick with foxgloves and bracken. Lights flickered in the heart of the wood and then were gone. "They're cocky enough about it now."

"They might have cause to regret it. Come on."

"But what about the lady?"

Nicholas paused in the act of alighting to look back at her. "Miss Durleigh, I fear you will have further cause to sanction me, for I must leave you alone here."

"Alone? Out here in the middle of nowhere you would leave me by myself?" She was horrified.

"I fear so."

"But why? What is your business in Ladywood?"

He raised her hand to his lips. "Patience, Miss Durleigh. For the moment it is more than enough that you are aware of my jaunts into Varangian's territory, without further burdening your ears with my reasons." He released her and jumped down.

She leaned from the open door to watch the two men slip over the stile and begin to move swiftly down the gully. There was no moonlight and in a moment or so they were lost from sight in the dark shadows of the wood. The wind rustled the trees and somehow the noise was chilling. The horses shifted slightly and the springs of the carriage squeaked. Something small and dark scuttled across the road and plunged into the long grass by the ditch, and she shivered, for it had looked like a rat. From deep in the woods came the sudden baying of hounds and the horses tossed their heads nervously. The barouche moved slightly before the brakes gripped. Anxiously, Jessica climbed down, going quickly to the horses to soothe them. The harness jingled, and she ignored the spoiling of her white gloves as she held the bridles and whispered gently. All around the breeze soughed through the branches and her heart was thundering as she stared at the dark, hidden shadows suddenly so menacing now that she was alone.

Abruptly, Ladywood was alive to shouting. More lanterns bobbed between the trees and a pistol shot rang out. The hounds renewed their noise and Jessica had difficulty holding the horses that were by now thoroughly alarmed.

A single horse moved up the incline from the direction of Applegarth. It was ridden at speed, careless of the ruts that lay in its path. Jessica watched, holding her breath, for she feared the rider must surely meet with an accident. Surprised, she recognized Jamie Pike. His hood had blown back from his face and as he glanced behind him she knew there could be no mistaking him. He did not see the carriage by the elderberry as he rode past, urging his horse toward the beech trees where he reined in, bending down to untether the horses there. He slapped their flanks and whistled shrilly, and in a moment the horses were scattering in all directions. Then Jamie urged his own mount along the boundary of Ladywood until he passed from sight over the brow of the hill toward the bay far below. Jessica had no time to ponder Jamie's activities, or the fact that the horse he rode would have done justice to any young blood in Hyde Park. The team was in no mood to be soothed and she had just about given up trying to hold them back, when suddenly heavy steps sounded by the stile.

"Sir Nicholas?" she cried, recognizing him as he half-carried, half-dragged the slumped body of the coachman. He bundled his companion over the stile and jumped after him, opening the carriage door and pushing Parr inside where he lay groaning.

"Get inside, Miss Durleigh, for there is no time to be lost." He seized her arm and pushed her toward the door.

He was already climbing into the driver's seat and she clambered into the cabin as quickly as she could, just managing to close the door as the whip cracked and the team strained forward down the long incline. She heard the hounds break from the woods to give chase, and she steadied herself against the seats as the barouche gathered momentum. Glancing down she saw bloodstains on her costly yellow silk, and she saw for the first time that Parr had a bullet wound in his left shoulder.

She took her handkerchief from her reticule and began to unbutton the coachman's coat. The blood oozed thickly over the black woolen cloth and she shuddered, for she had never liked blood and there was so much of it welling from the ugly wound. In a moment the handkerchief was soaked and useless, her gloves were bloody, and she looked in dismay at the yellow silk gown. Glancing up she saw that the barouche was lurching past the entrance to Applegarth and was now hurtling on towards Henbury. Behind, the hounds had given up the chase, but still Nicholas did not lessen the reckless speed.

She struggled to her feet and opened the small grille to speak to Nicholas. "Where are you going?"

"To Woodville House."

"But *I* cannot go there. Your mother and Rosamund would forbid me to enter."

"*I* am the master of Woodville House, Miss Durleigh, and my mother and sister-in-law will do as I say."

"What happened in Ladywood?"

"We almost got ourselves killed. I should have imagined that much to be obvious!"

"Yes, but why? What is all this about?" She closed her eyes as the barouche drove down toward the ford on the outskirts of the town. With a splash it passed over the foaming waters, then on to the cobbled street by the Feathers. Only then did Nicholas proceed steadily, so there could be no one to remark upon the wild speed of the Woodville barouche in the late hours of night.

Nicholas turned to look at her pale face peeping out through the grille. "How is he?"

"He is bleeding a lot. He should see a physician immediately."

"Cluffo Dowdeswell can do all that is necessary, Miss Durleigh."

She was aghast. "Cluffo is a groom, he knows horses, not men."

"Cluffo can be relied on to keep a still tongue in his head. Physicians cannot be so relied on."

"What is it that is so important you would risk Parr's life for it?"

He nodded. "I have managed to involve you in

97

my affairs, Miss Durleigh, and the least I can do is offer you an explanation. When we reach the house I will tell you everything you wish to know."

She sat back in the seat and looked down at the unconscious coachman. He moaned, and she crouched beside him immediately, forgetting the contemplation of Nicholas' revelations.

Chapter 12

"Tanner!" Nicholas was shouting the butler's name even before the barouche had halted.

Jessica looked up at the gables and latticed windows of the old Tudor mansion. Once she had been so welcome here; before. . . . She saw the door open and the old butler hurried out, staring in quick surprise at Nicholas on the driving seat.

"Sir Nicholas?"

"Have Parr taken inside and get Cluffo Dowdewsell out of his bed."

"Yes, Sir Nicholas." The butler asked no questions.

Jessica climbed down as two men came to drag the coachman from the carriage. Nicholas took her hand and led her into the house.

There was a smell of sandalwood in the hallway from the exotic, oriental chests standing against one wall. The oak staircase and gallery were as she remembered, and she looked up as a figure appeared there. It was Rosamund. Her face was flushed as if she had been hurrying, and her tousled hair was pushed beneath a white mobcap. She wore a jade-green dressing gown, but as she began to descend to the hall, Jessica noticed the green and gold stripes of her evening gown peeping from beneath it.

Rosamund looked coldly at Jessica. "Why have you brought her here, Nicholas?"

He sighed, loosening his cravat irritably. "I have my own reasons, my dear Rosamund, and they need not concern you. Get yourself back to your rooms and sleep on."

"I was not asleep. I was waiting for you so that I could apologize for my behavior at Varangian."

"Consider the apology unnecessary, Rosamund. I can hear my mother's bell ringing in her room. You had best go and set her mind at rest that nothing is wrong."

Rosamund raised her eyebrows for she was looking at Jessica's bloodstained gown. "Indeed? I find that hard to believe."

"Do as I ask, Rosamund. I implore you."

"Very well, Nicholas. I take it that I am to conceal from her the fact that Miss Durleigh is a guest here?"

"No, you may tell her if you wish. In fact, Rosamund, you can make amends to me for your lamentable conduct at Varangian by having the blue room prepared for Miss Durleigh."

Rosamund flushed. "I am not your servant, Nicholas."

"No, you are not. You are my sister and I

would ask my sister to help me. Don't nurse your injured pride so publicly, for it ill becomes you. Besides," and he smiled faintly, "the small matter of possessing my brother is not worth the breach in your friendship with Jessica. Philip was most certainly not worth scrapping over like a pair of alley cats. Now, Rosamund, if you please." He gestured toward the stairs.

Her face a dull red of embarrassment, Rosamund turned to go back up the stairs, her golden hair catching the light of an oil lamp as she looked back at Jessica for a moment.

Nicholas turned as the butler came from the direction of the kitchens. "Cluffo Dowdeswell has just arrived, Sir Nicholas. What shall I tell him?"

"That there has been an accident with my pistol. It went off half cocked. Let him believe that I have sent for him and not the doctor, because I do not desire any adverse comment to be passed concerning the matter."

"Yes, sir." Tanner bowed his head and went.

Nicholas pushed open the door of the sitting room and went inside. It was a dark, paneled room where a dying fire still glowed in the immense, Elizabethan hearth. Bowls of roses and honeysuckle stood on polished tables and a huge portrait of Philip stared down at Jessica from the chimney breast. She caught her breath as she looked at it, for she had not seen it before.

Nicholas grunted as he poured two glasses of Madeira. "My mother had it painted by Sir Thomas Lawrence, and nothing will content her but that it hangs there."

"He was so handsome."

"Aye, he was a dashing young blood and no mistake, but he was many other things as well, and that makes his great, personal beauty somewhat distasteful."

She said nothing.

He pushed a glass into her hand. "Do I take it from your silence that you begin to suspect I am right?"

"I loved him. I don't want to hear anything against him. Please." She raised her eyes to his face. "Please respect that wish, for it is not too much to ask."

He took her hand and pressed it to his lips. "If that is your desire, then I will stand by it. Tell me, Jessica, what is your relationship with Francis Varangian now?"

"Relationship? There is no relationship, Sir Nicholas. In fact, after tonight I doubt there is even the likelihood he would doff his hat to me in the street."

"Indeed?"

She nodded. "He said certain things that set a great wall between us."

"May I ask what happened?"

"You may not." She smiled reasonably.

He grinned at her. "Which puts me in my place firmly but politely."

"You were going to tell me about Ladywood."

"Ah, yes. Do sit down, Jessica, for until you do then I must remain standing and I have a great desire to rest my feet upon the fender before the fire. There are certain times when my mother's insistence upon a fire even in summertime appears to me to be an admirable trait in her make-up."

Jessica sat down in a high-backed settle close to the fire, and he sat beside her, leaning forward to look into the flames. His face was aglow in the dim light of the room, and the large emerald ring on his finger flashed as he raised his glass to drink.

"I must still ask that you honor your word to me and keep what I tell you a secret."

"I so promise."

"You know there is smuggling carried on in this neighborhood on a large scale?"

"Yes. Are you a smuggler, Sir Nicholas?"

"Now I am hurt beyond belief. Do I *look* like a smuggler?"

"You look perfectly capable of such an occupation, if I am to be honest with you, sir."

"I trust that was a compliment. No, Miss Durleigh, I am not a smuggler. I am a smuggler-catcher, or at least a would-be smuggler-catcher, for at the moment I am being singularly unsuccessful."

"You are a revenue man?"

"Not exactly. I am a government agent. You see, it is believed that the revenue men hereabouts are corrupt. I work alone with Parr."

She stared at him.

He smiled. "That is why I so desperately need your promise of silence. The merest breath of what I am up to would mean an end to me. And I do not say that last thing lightly."

"But if you know the smugglers' route, and you certainly know that they will use it on moonless nights, why is it you say you are unsuccessful? The ring could be broken at any time should you so desire it."

"I have not yet been able to catch the leader. I want Francis Varangian, Jessica."

103

"Francis? You jest, surely!"

He shook his head. "It is Varangian. I would swear it. For a long while the contraband was stored at the Widow Claybone's farm, but then one night it was moved to a new location, and Parr and I had a merry time tracking it down. Then we found the new hiding place in the old ruins in Ladywood. Right in the middle of Varangian land. And you will admit that the good Sir Francis spends a good deal of time chasing about the countryside at night."

"After poachers."

"Perhaps. Perhaps not."

"But it is ridiculous to imagine that Francis. . . ."

"Miss Durleigh, until recently Francis was, shall we say, hard up? He had reached the point of selling some perfectly good land on his western boundary. He made no great noise about it, but I found out through my land agent. Then it transpired that a good-sized herd of his fine cattle was on the market, too. Varangian would never have done either of those two things unless he was desperately short of money. Then, just when Philip died, I remember, he seemed affluent once more, and it was at about that time that the ring began to operate. As I see it, Varangian was virtually penniless and decided to swell his fast-emptying coffers by smuggling from the safe bay below Ladywood. It is a perfect spot for such activities."

Jessica's fingers ran nervously over the cold diamonds in her necklace. Could he be right? She closed her eyes and for a moment she saw Francis' contorted face as he had accused her and Philip of blackmail. She looked at Nicholas' profile suddenly. "But if you are right, why then did he set his hounds on the smugglers the night you released me from the trap?"

"I think he caught wind that the wood was being watched. It was a clever plot to throw anyone off his trail."

"Or it could be he was indeed after poachers and fell on the smugglers by accident."

"That could be so, but I am disinclined to believe it."

"And tonight?"

"Tonight the hounds caught our scent and gave the alarm. But for that I would have got the proof I needed of Varangian's involvement."

She leaned forward to put her full glass upon a small table. "I wish now that I had not asked you to tell me," she murmured.

"I certainly owed you an explanation."

"Nonetheless. . . ."

"Jessica, you must not have a conscience on Varangian's behalf, for if he is indeed guilty, then capture is no more than he deserves."

She lowered her eyes to the stains on her gown. No more than he deserved? But if he was driven to it by blackmail? Faintly, she realized that for the first time she was beginning to doubt Philip. She glanced up at the portrait and felt sad.

Nicholas stood, smiling at her. "I hope you forgive me for upending your evening so much, I realize Woodville House is probably the last place in Henbury you would wish to spend a night."

"It was not to be helped, Sir Nicholas."

The butler appeared in the doorway. "Miss Rosamund asked me to inform you that the blue room is now ready, Sir Nicholas."

"Thank you, Tanner. You may retire now. Is Parr all right?"

"Yes, sir. He is sleeping now. Cluffo was able to cleanse the wound and bandage it securely."

"And Cluffo was satisfied with the explanation?"

"He gave no sign to the contrary, Sir Nicholas."

"Good night then, Tanner."

"Good night, Sir Nicholas."

The door closed.

"Well, Jessica, I think I should not keep you from your sleep a moment longer."

"I feel so unsettled that I doubt I shall manage to sleep at all." She rose, tightening the strings of her reticule, for she had been toying with them throughout. "What of Rosamund, though? I mean, if you are right about Francis. . . ."

"Rosamund will have to weather the scandal again, as she weathered one once before."

"But if she loves him?"

"Even so, for I have seen no sign that he has even noticed her existence, so perhaps we talk of an hypothesis."

"You know that she loves him, and so, I gather, do others in Henbury. What then does your mother think of it?"

Nicholas smiled. "My mother does not know, for by all the powers I have taken great care that the truth is concealed from her. Philip's memory is something my mother treasures and upholds more fiercely than anything, and if she thought that his widow loved another man there would be the most terrible altercation."

"I can well imagine."

"No doubt." He took her hand, turning the palm to his lips.

"Don't." Disturbed, she took her hand away.

"Why? Because I am his brother?"

She looked uncomfortably at him. His action had perplexed her. When she looked at him she was reminded of Philip, yet he was unlike his dead brother in almost every way.

He smiled, turning away. "Good night, Miss Durleigh."

"Good night."

Chapter 13

The sunlight was bright, falling in a shaft of sunbeams across Jessica's face. Her eyes opened sleepily and she stared across the room at the unfamiliar blue silk wallpaper and the bowl of delphiniums standing in the corner on the lilac and white carpet. A shadow moved across the sunlight and she sat up abruptly. Someone was sitting on the window seat.

"Rosamund?"

Rosamund smiled uncertainly, her long pale hands clasped neatly in her lap, her golden hair piled expertly into tumbling Grecian locks that peeped precisely from beneath her lacy mobcap. "Jessica."

"What do you want?" Jessica pulled the brocade coverlet around her bare shoulders.

"To end our differences."

"Why? Oh, I don't mean to sound so distrustful, but you must admit this change of heart has come somewhat abruptly."

"I know." Rosamund reddened uncomfortably and her hands moved nervously over the sprigged muslin of her gown. "I was being churlish."

"With good cause. I have given you little reason to like me, I know that."

"It was something Nicholas said last night—about Philip not being worth the breach in our friendship. He was right, you know. Or perhaps you do not know, for no doubt my husband showed only his charming and attentive side to you. He loved you dearly in his way."

"As I did him."

"Then continue to remember him kindly, for it can do no harm now."

"So mellow suddenly?"

"You know I felt nothing but dislike for him. I know well enough you considered that before going with him. I love Francis. Did you know?"

Jessica nodded. "And how does he feel?"

"Oh, would that I knew. You know how he is. Even if he was consumed with desire for me he would say nothing. First of all, I was married to Philip and Francis was betrothed to you. Then Philip died and I am a widow in fresh weeds." She smiled, glancing down at the dark green embroidery on the pale cream muslin. "Or at least, I should be. But I cannot pretend to mourn a man I hated."

"And I would mourn him but have no right. We are a pair, aren't we?"

"I must explain my behavior toward you, Jess. You see, I had forgiven you for the blow to my pride. I felt no animosity toward you, for you kept Philip in London and I was not forced to be polite to him or to. . . . Well, I saw little of him, shall we say. When he died I thought that, at last, Francis might notice me, for I was determined I would come before his attention until he was *forced* to notice me. But you came back, Jess. That was like a blow across the face to me. I knew Francis had asked you to marry him because he loved you, not because the match was arranged or because it was a prudent marriage. You were virtually penniless, a farmer's daughter, and he was the greatest landowner in north Somerset. For him, at least, it was a love match. Can you understand how I felt when I knew you would be in Henbury once more? Alone and, no doubt, as beautiful as ever. I could not cope with my jealousy, and I freely admit it."

"I don't want Francis. I never have. I was grievously at fault in ever accepting his proposal in the first place. You *had* to marry Philip, for it was your father's wish. There was no such onus on me, and yet I chose to accept Francis' suit."

"The prospect of such a marriage must have been a great temptation, and he is so gentle and kind." Rosamund lowered her eyes shyly.

For a moment Jessica saw Francis as he had been in the study at Varangian. What if Nicholas' suspicions were correct? She did not look at Rosamund. "Your way to him is clear, Rosamund, for I offer no threat. I do assure you that he does not love me. He may have once, but certainly not now. Does that reassure you a little?"

Rosamund's eyes filled with sudden tears and Jessica stared at the expression of guilt on her face. Guilt? With a quick breath Rosamund seemed about to say something more when a new sound was heard outside the bedroom door.

A stick tap-tapped on the polished wooden floor and Rosamund went pale. "Lady Amelia!" she whispered, getting nervously to her feet.

The door opened and the old lady came in. She was dressed from head to toe in the deepest mourning, her black mobcap adorned with long weepers. Beads of jet flashed on her thin chest, and her heavy crepe skirts rustled as she crossed the room to stand by the bed. She glanced coldly at Rosamund. "You may go now, miss."

"Yes, Lady Amelia."

The sharp bright eyes moved over the sprigged muslin. "You will wear black, madam. I insist upon it."

Rosamund said nothing, but her chin came up defiantly as she went to the door, closing it quietly behind her.

"Why are you here, Miss Durleigh?"

"Force of circumstances, Lady Amelia, and most certainly not choice."

"There is no need to be flippant, missy. I have given orders for the gig to be made ready. You may leave the moment you are dressed."

"Very well."

The old lady walked to the window to look out over the ornamental gardens with their high, decorative hedges and pools. "My son should not have brought you here. I am angered that he saw fit to do so. What is it about you, Miss Durleigh? Nicholas associates with you for one evening and comes home with the coachman wounded by his

112

pistol. Do you begin to set your sights at my elder son now?"

Jessica smiled dryly. "If this is the direction of your conversation, Lady Amelia, then you have chosen it and not I. I set my sights at Francis Varangian, not at Philip. Your sons are perfectly capable of seeking out for themselves that which they want. I know that to be so of Philip, and I should imagine that Sir Nicholas is the same. You play them false by suggesting they are susceptible to the wiles of a mere woman."

"A whore, Miss Durleigh, a whore."

"You may insult me if you choose, for I am most certainly a prisoner in this bed until you leave."

Lady Amelia turned quickly to look at her. "I despise you, missy, as I have never despised another human being in my life. Until he became so besotted with you, Philip was everything any mother could desire in a son. But you changed him. He became secretive and scheming, treating all and sundry with contempt, viciousness even, and spending far more money than he could ever have come by legally. To keep you, no doubt. You have a lot to answer for, Miss Durleigh. Now get you from this house and never return again. Do I make myself clear?"

"Perfectly." Jessica stared at the Jacobean flowers embroidered on the coverlet, her face a dull red, and she felt cold and sick at the old woman's hatred.

The stick tapped around the edge of the carpet, and at the door Lady Amelia paused. "Where did

113

he get his money?" she asked slowly, watching Jessica carefully.

"I do not know. *I* trusted him in every way and felt no need to inquire of such things."

The thin lips tightened angrily at the barb, but Jessica sensed the old woman had somehow relaxed, that her answer to the question had in some way settled an anxiety.

When the door closed at last, Jessica slipped from the bed and picked up the diamond necklace from its hiding place beneath the pillow. The stones winked and glittered in the sunbeams from the window as she looked at it. The money had come from Francis Varangian, she knew that now. But why? *Why?* Everything seemed set to fit into place, like pieces of a jigsaw puzzle that insist upon being completed. And the finished picture she knew she would not like.

She slipped the necklace into her reticule and picked up the bloodstained, yellow silk gown.

Chapter 14

The traveling rug in the gig covered the bloodstains, but even so Jessica was aware of the strange sight she made in her evening clothes as the gig drove smartly through the market square. She stared resolutely at the pony's ears and refused to glance to either side. Cluffo Dowdeswell slowed the pony's pace as they reached the lane on the other side of the ford. Now the gig moved at a walking pace and she was conscious of the man's interest in her.

"You was with Sir Nicholas last night, was you?"

"What are you insinuating, Cluffo?"

"Nowt, nowt at all. I was just thinking of Harry Parr's accident, that's all."

"Oh."

"How did it happen?"

She looked innocently at him. "I would not know, for I was not there at the time. I merely accompanied Sir Nicholas from Varangian and was with the unfortunate Mr. Parr for a while. Hence the bloodstains that, no doubt, you have noticed.

"Couldn't help but notice, could I? Red do have a habit of showing up on yeller."

"How observant you are."

"Oh, you're proper uppity now, aren't you? Farmer Durleigh's stuck-up daughter."

"You are as insolent now as ever you were, Cluffo. I wonder if Sir Nicholas would hear your words so kindly."

"I didn't mean owt by it. 'Tis just hard to forget as how you was a little girl what liked to help me with the horses."

"Until you got drunk once too often and overturned the wagon and so lost your position. You were lucky to get yourself in at Woodville House."

"Ah. 'Tis that scrumpy, it do go to my head."

"Cider gets the blame, does it? Not the willing hand that raises the glass time and time again."

"You'm sharp-tongued, and all. Did you see the kerfuffle in Ladywood last night?"

She met his gaze. "Kerfuffle?"

"Aye."

"What do you mean?"

"I hears there was a rumpus there again, and I wondered if'n you saw it when you passed."

"What sort of rumpus?" she asked, avoiding the question.

"Oh, shooting and shouting and hounds. A general uproar."

116

"Really? I do hope Tamsin was all right at Applegarth all by herself."

"She knows where you was, anyhow, for I was sent to push a note through the letterbox for her to find the minute she woke up this morning. It seemed quiet enough when I was there. Reckon she'd gone to bed."

"I wonder you didn't knock the door to find out," remarked Jessica dryly.

The thrust went over his head, for he did not even glance at her as he urged the lazy pony on toward Applegarth. The sunlight cast dappled shadows across the lane and the birds were singing merrily in the trees. Then a figure hurried toward them, appearing suddenly from a path between the trees. It was Jamie, running for all he was worth, with Nipper loping along beside him.

Cluffo reined in. "Mornin', Jamie."

Jamie halted, leaning breathlessly on the gig. "Cluffo. Miss Jess." He tipped his hat politely, his dark eyes resting momentarily on the bloodstains.

"Is something wrong, Jamie?" She felt vaguely alarmed but did not know why.

"Yes, Miss Jess. There's been someone break into Applegarth. Tamsin's had a blow on the head, but she seems all right. I was running into Henbury to fetch the physician, or the apothecary."

"Someone broke in?" she repeated, staring at him.

"Aye, but Tamsin seems to think nothing was stolen. But 'tis in a real mess."

117

"Oh, Cluffo, hurry and get me back there."

Jamie stepped away from the gig. "She found the note to say you were at Woodville House with Sir Nicholas," he said, smiling slightly.

Cluffo leaned forward, looking earnestly at the shepherd. "She were with Harry Parr, him as got his self shot last night."

Jamie's clear eyes moved to her face thoughtfully. "Sir Nicholas' coachman?"

She nodded. "Cluffo attended his wound."

"Not the physician? Why so secret?"

She remembered what Nicholas had said. "Well, I believe it was an accident involving Sir Nicholas. Perhaps he chose to avoid tittle-tattle."

"Ah, that's the way of the gentry, right enough." Jamie tipped his hat again and watched the gig rattle away down the lane between the trees.

Jessica's heart was thundering now as she sought the first glimpse of the cottage. Suddenly she remembered the fine horse Jamie had ridden the night before. If he possessed such a horse, why then did he choose to run all the way into Henbury on so urgent an errand? Or was it perhaps the beast he used when he held up mail coaches on the Taunton road? It was certainly a mount to remember once seen.

"We'm there, Miss Jessica. I'll set you down at the gate here and go back to take Jamie into Henbury. I'll still be quicker than he is on foot."

Jessica ran through the grass beneath the cider-apple trees and threw open the front door. The clean, tidy kitchen that was Tamsin's pride and joy was in a shambles. Everything had been knocked from the shelves, the fire had been riddled and the ashes tossed over the tiled floor, and all the flour had been emptied from the barrel and then walked through so that footprints covered the raddling. A glance into the drawing room revealed similar chaos.

"Miss Jess?" Tamsin came into the kitchen, a dustpan and brush in her hand. "Oh, Miss Jess." Her plump face puckered and she burst into tears.

A short while later the kettle was boiling on a newly-lit fire and Jessica pushed a fresh cup of tea across the table. "Drink this, Tamsin, and dry your eyes. It isn't the end of the world."

"Not quite."

"Is your head aching?"

"Like someone was inside with a mallet. Reckon I'll be right glad to see the physician."

"When he's been, you must go back to your bed and have a good rest. You'll soon feel better. But tell me what happened?"

"Well, if you looks in the drawing room you'll see how they got in, for there's a broken pane in the back window. That's what I heard. Well, first off, I was woke by the noise in Ladywood when Sir Francis and the poachers had another set-to. I was lying there wondering when you would be back when I heard the glass breaking. It weren't much of a noise and I wouldn't have heard it at all if I'd been asleep. I reckoned it must be that tortie cat come in through the larder window for something for her kittens, and so I went down to shoo her off. My heaven, did I see stars for a second. Something hit the back of my head and I went out like a candle. Next thing I knew it were daylight and I was lying there at the foot of the stairs and everything was like you sees it now."

119

"You didn't know until this morning that I was at Woodville House?"

"No. The note hadn't come when I went to bed and I found it when I come round. Why?"

"Well, Cluffo Dowdeswell brought it." Jessica glanced around at the mess.

"You reckon as how Cluffo might've done this? No, Miss Jess, not him. He be a crafty old rogue, and no mistake, but breaking in and causing all this damage ain't in his line. He'm more of a poacher and a smuggler, is that one."

"A smuggler?"

"Cluffo? Oh, aye, he'm always ready for such like. You ask his wife Dolly. I tell you, she've got two barrels of good cognac in her cellar. Cognac! And him a groom, that's all. She give me the wink once. Cluffo is one of the ring."

Suddenly the old groom's questions about Harry Parr's accident took a more sinister meaning. Did Cluffo suspect Nicholas? She thought of Jamie riding to scatter Francis' horses. Was the shepherd one of the ring, too? She stood as she heard the gig returning. "Here they come with the physician." She opened the door as the gig came to a standstill. Jamie, worn out with all his running, lolled in the seat with Nipper on his lap, and Cluffo climbed down to tether the pony. The physician pushed past Jessica and went to attend to Tamsin.

Jamie got down wearily, setting Nipper on the ground. "Reckon that's a job well done, Miss Jess."

"Thank you so much, Jamie. Will you have some Madeira? It's all we have here but you are welcome."

He nodded. "Reckon that'll go down a treat.

Cluffo, you'd best get yourself back to Woodville House."

"Aye. See you in three days then, Jamie."

Jessica glanced from one to the other. "Three days?" she asked innocently.

Jamie grinned and put his finger to his lips. "A spot of poaching, Miss Jess. We've a fancy for some good venison."

He followed her into the cottage where the physician was finishing bandaging Tamsin's head. He closed his bag and pointed to a small phial on the table.

"She's to have that when I've gone, Miss Durleigh. It's laudanum and will help her to sleep. Rest and quiet is all that's needed. She's had a bit of a shock, no more."

"Thank you, sir."

"That'll be nine shillings and sixpence, if you please, Miss Durleigh."

Jessica took her purse from the shelf and counted the coins into the man's hand. When he had gone she mixed the laudanum and ushered Tamsin up the stairs.

Jamie was waiting by the range, holding his hands to the warmth. Nipper whined and wagged his tail as Jessica came down the stairs. Jamie looked at the bloodstains. "Harry Parr bled like a stuck pig then?"

"He did indeed."

"Where did it happen, Jess?"

She took the Madeira from the cupboard and carefully poured two glasses. "Where did what happen?"

"The shooting?"

121

"I did not see the shooting, Jamie. Is that enough wine?"

He nodded, his dark face clever. "You left the ball early they say."

"They have a lot to say. How did you know?"

"The postboy from the Feathers. He went back to Varangian for you and was told you had left with Sir Nicholas."

"That is correct. I went back to Woodville House with him."

"A link back to Master Philip is he, Jess?" he asked softly.

"Don't presume on our friendship so much, Jamie. It is none of your business why I accompanied Sir Nicholas."

"No, but I can guess for he's a good-looking chap. Single and all. Not so much of a way with him as his brother, but comely enough."

"Jamie!"

"I mean no harm, Jess, for I've always liked you. You had a fair pair of ankles and I recall watching for a glimpse of them in the schoolyard. I've a weakness for pretty ankles and so I forgive you all your sins."

"My sins! You have a nerve, Jamie Pike."

"What do you mean?"

"I mean the mail bag in my stable loft."

He put down his glass. "Why should I know anything about that?"

She told him of having seen him. "So don't preach to me about sin, Jamie."

"You knew that, and yet you didn't tell on me to the magistrate?"

"I remember holding hands with you on Sun-

122

days in church, Jamie, and I could never betray you."

He bent forward and kissed her cheek gently. "Thank you, Jess Durleigh. I reckon I owes you something now."

"You owe me nothing."

"Oh, I do. I'm in your debt and there's a way I can repay it."

"How?"

"By telling you who did this here last night."

"You know?"

"I reckon so, though I couldn't prove it. I was out and about last night looking after some sickly sheep. I came up past here and saw a horse tethered secretly by your stables."

She sipped her wine. She knew well enough that Jamie had been abroad the previous night. Had she not see him herself. "Whose horse was it?"

"Miss Rosamund's."

She almost dropped the glass. "You jest!"

"No. I saw her. Not going into the cottage or anything like that. Just standing, looking toward it as if undecided."

Jessica turned away. She saw again Rosamund's flushed face as she had appeared at the head of the stairs in that jade-green dressing gown. She had still been wearing her evening gown underneath and had looked as if she had been hurrying. Had she returned to the big house only moments before the barouche? "Could you be mistaken, Jamie?"

"No. And Cluffo found her horse back at Woodville House. It was lathered up a treat when he put his own nag there to go and look to Harry Parr. You don't have to look far for a motive, do you?"

"Oh, Jamie." She bit her lip, easy tears filling her eyes. Only that morning she had thought all was well between her and Rosamund once more.

Jamie put his arms around her and held her gently. "Don't take on, or I'll wish I'd held my tongue. I thought you should know, though."

She leaned her head wearily against his shoulder. He pushed her gently into a chair and crouched before her, his hands enfolding hers. "Don't let it swamp you, for you're better than all of them. Get out of Henbury because it'll do you no good to stay. I'm going the minute I've got all the money I need. And a good pair of heels I'll show Somerset and all."

"Where shall you go?"

"America."

"Do they have mail coaches there, too, then?" she asked, trying to smile.

He grinned. "Reckon so."

She sat quietly in the kitchen after he had gone. She could hear the slow ticking of the grandfather clock in the drawing room, and the shifting of the new fire in the range. She looked around at the destruction of her home and then she buried her face in her hands.

Chapter 15

She did not hear Nicholas arriving. He pushed open the door and looked inside in amazement.

"Miss Durleigh?"

She started, sitting up from where she had slumped her face on her arms on the table. Her eyes were red from weeping and there was nothing she could do to conceal the fact. "Sir Nicholas?"

He came in, flinging his tall hat on the table and taking off his fine leather gloves. "What happened?"

She told him, omitting the fact that she suspected Rosamund to be the culprit.

"Was anything taken?"

"I don't think so. The only thing of value I possess was on my person."

"The necklace?"

"Yes."

"And Miss Davey?"

"She's upstairs. The physician prescribed some laudanum. Whoever broke in hit her on the head. But she will be all right, I'm assured."

"And you?" he said gently.

"Merely shaken."

His riding boots squeaked slightly as he went to the window to look out. "I came the moment my mother told me what she had done. I am sorry she treated you so appallingly."

"She felt justified."

"You were my guest. She should not have spoken as she did."

"I had forgotten. This terrible mess had put it from my mind."

"You are too kind."

"No." She smiled a little. "I gave Lady Amelia as fine a verbal set-to as she'd had in a long time, I fancy."

"For her that would be a novel experience. To make amends for all you were forced to endure, though, I shall send some maids over from Woodville House to tidy up here."

"There is no need."

"I insist."

"Then I accept. Sir Nicholas, I think Cluffo Dowdeswell may be one of the smugglers. He drove me back here this morning, and he was most interested in your coachman's accident. He asked me if I had seen anything in Ladywood last night, and when he asked he knew that I had been with you. I wondered if he was suspicious of you."

"He was bound to be nosy about the accident—it was inevitable."

"Nonetheless. . . ."

"I shall be more circumspect in my dealings with him. I am honored that you sought to warn me." His eyes were dark.

"I would not wish any harm to come to you."

He came nearer, bending to cup her face in his hands. "Do I detect any gentleness in your heart, Jessica?"

"I pray not," she whispered, "for it would be so *unsuitable.*"

His lips were warm as he kissed her, and she closed her eyes. Suddenly she stood, moving away from him. "Don't, please."

"Because of Philip? Answer me, Jessica, for I must know."

"I don't know, Nicholas. Don't you see? I don't know if it is because you look so like him, or if it is you that I. . . . I am confused and uncertain of myself. So much has happened in so short a while."

"The devil, Jessica! What it is to envy a ghost, for that is surely what I do now. You loved him in life and now you love his memory almost as much."

"Would you think any more of me were I to forget him so quickly?"

He straightened. "No. But I feel bitter that a man like Philip could so keep his hold on you."

"Am I really the only one still wearing blinkers concerning him?"

He nodded. "And my mother—although I fancy she refuses to remove the blinkers although she knows she should."

"She blames me for what he was."

127

"She would blame anyone. There must be a scapegoat."

"But how could I not have seen anything of this other side that I am continually assured did exist?"

"Love is blind."

"He was everything I could ever have wished for, you know."

"You would have discovered the truth in the end. Even Francis Varangian refused to visit Woodville House while my brother was alive. He did not set foot over the threshhold once."

"And now?"

"Now he has called. I believe to see Rosamund. He was there after breakfast this morning."

"She will be glad."

"I could have wished he had remained away under the circumstances. If I can, I will trap him, and that will not help my sister-in-law."

"Does Lady Amelia know he was there?"

"No, she remained in her rooms."

"That is just as well."

"Indeed. But we have digressed, have we not?" He turned her toward him. "I cannot leave matters between us in so unsatisfactory a state."

She took his hand and rested it against her cheek. "You are being honest with me and I am trying to do the same for you. I like you. I like you very much, although I never would have dreamed that I would."

He drew her closer. "That is sufficient for me for the moment," he murmured, kissing her again.

In spite of herself she returned the kiss, slipping her arms around him to hold him tightly. The blood rushed through her veins.

He drew away, smiling. "I shall exorcise that persistent ghost yet."

"Perhaps there is too much of a past, Nicholas."

"No." He picked up his hat and drew his gloves on slowly. "No, I will not believe that. I shall send some maids to clear up then."

"Yes."

He paused before her, looking into her wide green eyes. "I am very close to loving you, Jessica. You know that, don't you?"

She nodded.

She watched him ride away, leaning her head against the cool glass of the window. The roses around the doorway bobbed and danced in the breeze and she could smell their sweet perfume. A pigeon fluttered down among Tamsin's vegetables and she went to the door, clapping her hands noisily. She looked at the well-worn path leading into Ladywood where the heavy green leaves folded over it as if to hide it from sight. In three days were Cluffo and Jamie to meet for poaching as they said? Or, were they smuggling?

She looked back to where Nicholas had ridden away. How much danger was he in? She closed her eyes, remembering how he had kissed her.

By nightfall the maids had cleaned the cottage from top to bottom, and Tamsin slept on in her bed, oblivious to the clatter of brushes and dishes that went on all round her throughout the long summer afternoon.

As the sun set at last beyond Ladywood, Jessica

lay in the mulberry-hung bed and looked through the small latticed window. She saw Francis' scarlet curricle skim up the incline towards Varangian. Had he been to visit Rosamund again? She turned to look up at the bed hangings. What had Philip been blackmailing him for? She closed her eyes to sleep, but her head was spinning with unanswered questions.

Chapter 16

"Tamsin, you should not be bending about with that vegetable patch. Your head will begin to ache again."

"Weeds don't respect people's headaches, Miss Jess."

Jessica sat down on the grass and began to remove the leaves from the bunch of sweet williams she had gathered. "Have you seen Dolly Dowdeswell lately?"

"Aye. This morning in the market. Why?"

"I just wondered. Could we not get some cognac, too?"

"Miss Jess. I'm ashamed of you."

"Cognac is very nice in coffee."

"London habits."

"Some Henbury habits are doubtful."

"True enough. Well, I doubt as us'll get any

cognac now for the ring is ending after tonight, so Dolly says. Seems like there's trouble among the revenue men, rumors about nets closing in and such like. There's one more load coming ashore tonight and then that be it."

Jessica turned a sweet william in her hand, looking at the delicate rosettes of pink and white. One more night and then Nicholas would be safe from detection.

Tamsin wiped her forehead and straightened, rubbing her back. "There be something on your mind, I can tell."

"Would it be very reprehensible to fall in love with Sir Nicholas?"

"It'd be a sight more in line than when you went off with his brother." Tamsin stepped carefully over the line of carrots and sat beside her. "You and Sir Nicholas then?"

"I think so."

"That be what I might call moving at a fair gallop, if'n you don't mind me saying so."

"I know."

"And still it do seem right?"

"Yes."

"Then happen, it *is* right. But you'll meet a sight of opposition from most directions, you know that?"

"Yes."

"And you can get over losing Master Philip so quick?"

With a jolt, Jessica realized she had thought very little about Philip from the moment Nicholas had kissed her. "Yes."

"And good riddance, too, for he were a bad lot, a very bad lot."

132

"I begin to know that."

"Ah, well, that were inevitable. His brother be the better man. There ain't much wrong with Sir Nicholas Woodville. Miss Jess, did you know as how Sir Francis and Miss Rosamund have been stepping out together?"

"Well. . . ."

"Only when I were in Henbury it were the regular talk. Seems there was a terrible scene with Lady Amelia who right enough don't approve of such things when Miss Rosamund should still be wearing black. She've confined Miss Rosamund to the house for the time being, and if'n Miss Rosamund wants to keep a roof over her head, then she has to do as she's told."

"Poor Rosamund."

"Well, her knew what her was doing when her went out with Sir Francis."

"I hope it goes well for her now."

"Talk of Old Bogey and he's sure to appear. Look."

Jessica turned toward the driveway to see the Woodville barouche drive in from the Henbury road. Inside sat Rosamund, her face pale and troubled.

Slowly, Jessica stood, taking a deep breath. It would be hard to be pleasant to Rosamund after what Jamie had revealed about her presence at Applegarth on the night of the ball.

The barouche came to a halt by the yellow door, and Jessica waited as the coachman opened the door for Rosamund to alight.

"Rosamund?"

"Jessica." There was a tremble in the soft voice.

133

"I came to see if you would accompany me on a drive to Henbury Lake."

Jessica was taken aback. "Please come inside."

"No. No, I will wait here." Rosamund glanced uneasily at the cottage.

"Then I will put on my pelisse and come now."

"Thank you."

"Surely it is I who should be thanking you for this unexpected pleasure."

Rosamund shook her head. "I come on a purely selfish errand, for I have something most special to ask of you."

Tamsin wiped her hand on her apron. "Miss Rosamund, did I hear you say Henbury Lake?"

"Yes, Tamsin, why?"

"Begging your pardon, miss, but could I perhaps beg a ride with you to the gates of Woodville House, for you must pass that way. Our pony be at the farrier's."

"Yes, of course. But what business have you there?"

"It's on account of Harry Parr, Miss Rosamund, I hear as how he got his self shot and as he's my mother's cousin, and family like. . . ."

"You wish to visit with him?"

"If I may, for 'tis only polite."

"But, of course. I am sure he would be pleased to see you. Tanner informs me that Parr is most fractious and frets at being confined to his bed."

"Oh, that be Harry Parr all right, a regular terror when he's not well. I've some honey and a batch set aside to take for him, and a jar of elderberry wine from last fall." Tamsin hurried in to fill a basket and was waiting in the barouche when Jessica at last came out with her

134

hair pinned beneath a straw bonnet and her navy blue pelisse buttoned tidily.

The barouche had been cleaned thoroughly inside. Jessica sat opposite Rosamund, looking down at the well-scrubbed carpeting where not a sign of blood remained. At the gates of the big house, Tamsin climbed out.

"Miss Jess, I reckon as how little Jinks will have been reshod by the time I've done with my visiting, so happen I'll be back at Applegarth afore you."

"Yes, Tamsin. Give my good wishes to your cousin."

"I will. And thank you again, Miss Rosamund."

Rosamund inclined her head, then tapped the front of the barouche and it moved off again. Jessica looked through the great iron gates hoping to see Nicholas, but she saw nothing except the trees lining the curved driveway.

"Well, Rosamund? You have something to ask of me?"

"Yes. It concerns Francis and myself. You have heard what has happened?"

"I have heard something, yes."

"Well, most probably you have heard the truth. Lady Amelia will throw me out if I insist upon seeing him again. Jess, I have nowhere to go if she does. I would go to Francis, wearing his ring or not, but he will not hear of it. He says he cannot marry me yet, as he has doubts that he will be master of Varangian much longer."

"Francis said that?"

"Yes." Rosamund looked away suddenly. "I would go to him, with or without his fortune."

"But what can I do to help?"

135

"You can offer me a home."

"At Applegarth?"

Again the sliding, unhappy eyes. "Yes."

"You are sure that that is what you want?"

"Yes. Oh, yes. Jess, I have a terrible confession to make." Tears filled the lovely eyes.

"That you were the one who broke into the cottage?"

"How did you know that?" gasped Rosamund, turning even paler than before.

"Shall we say that a little bird told me?"

"You knew, and still greet me as a friend?"

"I hoped perhaps you would tell me, and explain why you did it. It was very difficult to look gently at you, I do assure you."

"I was looking for something, something I thought must be in your possession. You see, Francis was being blackmailed by Philip. Did you know?"

"Francis told me himself. He accused me of being party to it."

"Yes. Francis has not told me anything concerning it. I knew only because I once accompanied Philip to Varangian, and overheard them speaking together. Philip told Francis he would continue to demand payment as he still had possession of the note, and while he did so Francis was caught."

"Note?"

"That was the word used. So I knew that something existed that gave Philip a hold over Francis, although I still do not know what. I could tell it had begun again since your return to Henbury and, like Francis, I put two and two together to make five. I saw you at the ball and left, fully

136

intending to ride back to Applegarth to make a search for the note that I believed you to have. I did not know Tamsin Davey was living with you. I panicked when I heard her get out of bed, for I knew she would see me and recognize me if I tried to escape, so I hit her with the teapot."

"Her precious silver teapot? Rosamund, I am surprised at you."

"I am horrified and disgusted with myself. I knew as I was searching that you could not possibly be guilty of so foul a crime as blackmail. And not to Francis of all people, for he had never done you any harm. Indeed, when you left him, he alone in Henbury spoke out in your defense. I was in such a quandary that I left the cottage and stood by my horse, wondering what to do about Tamsin who was still lying at the foot of the stairs where I had left her. I knew she was not badly hurt, but my conscience was so very terrible. Then such a commotion broke out in Ladywood that I mounted and left without further ado. I had only just left my horse in the stables at Woodville House and had time to get to my rooms when I heard the barouche returning. Can you ever forgive me?"

"You have forgiven me much, how then can I refuse to do the same for you. Of course, I forgive you, and, of course, you may come to Applegarth. Only. . . ."

"Yes?"

"How does Sir Nicholas feel over this matter of you and Francis?"

"He has said nothing at all, except to once ask me to reconsider."

Jessica looked out at the passing hedges. The

137

sky blue waters of the lake glinted through the lacing branches. If Rosamund burned her bridges by coming to Applegarth, and then Francis was indeed caught as the ringleader of the smugglers. . . . But there was only tonight to survive. "Where will Sir Nicholas be tonight?"

"I have no idea. Why ever do you ask?"

"No reason, really."

"Did you wish to see him then?"

A way seemed to open before Jessica. "Yes. Yes, I think I should perhaps speak to him before anything is done." Yes, and keep him at Applegarth for as long as possible so that he could not watch over anything in Ladywood.

Rosamund looked a little miffed. "I do not see that his opinion makes any difference."

"To you, no. But to me it makes a great deal of difference."

Rosamund's eyes cleared. "You and Nicholas?"

"I have a great tenderness for him, certainly."

"You will have to get past the dragon."

"Lady Amelia?"

"*My* conduct is cutting her to the very quick. I shudder to imagine what she would do were Nicholas to seek your hand."

"Oh, I do not think it has come to that pass yet, if indeed it comes to it at all."

"You would be his mistress?"

"No."

"You will hold out for a ring then?"

"No. I merely know that I will be no man's mistress again. But I do not seek to marry him. I know only that I enjoy his company a great deal and look forward to the time when I shall see him next."

"Then that is surely a firm platform from which to begin."

"It merely means that I like him and would set matters right with him *before* you leave the big house."

"Shall I tell him you wish to speak with him?"

"Yes. Ask him if he will come to Applegarth tonight."

"He may construe that as a certain kind of invitation, Jessica."

Perplexed, Jessica lowered the window to breathe the flower-scented air. "Well, I cannot go to see him at Woodville House. He *must* come to the cottage."

"Meet him somewhere in Henbury, for that would surely be the most seemly solution."

Without explaining that she wished to make certain Nicholas was kept away from Ladywood that night, Jessica could say no more, so she changed the subject as the barouche rumbled to a halt by the little landing stage where the rowing boats were moored. High on the hill they could see Varangian Hall, standing proud of its vast parklands on the great hill overlooking the sea.

Rosamund stood on the jetty looking up at the house. "Do you think he will lose it somehow?"

"I don't know, Rosamund."

"Someone has that cursed note—I know that must be so!"

"But who? Philip's papers have been gone through by the Woodville lawyers now, and nothing has come to light or you would know of it."

"I know that the blackmail has begun again."

139

"Yes, from a letter Philip sent before he died—a letter that was in the stolen mail bag."

"But. . . ."

"Francis chose not to believe me. Unless, as you say, someone else has the note."

They looked at each other.

"But who?" asked Rosamund at last.

"I don't know." Jessica pushed the prow of a boat with her toe and it dipped on the wavelets. "Can I come to Applegarth tomorrow?"

"So quickly?"

"I have decided that I want Francis and nothing will stand in my way."

"You may come when you wish, Rosamund, for you are very welcome."

"And what of Nicholas?"

"I will have to face that if and when it comes."

"There are rain clouds coming inland, look. Shall we go back now?"

They climbed back into the waiting barouche and soon were swaying back along the lane towards Henbury. Jessica looked up at the darkening skies where the clouds were gathering with alarming swiftness. But there was no wind, nothing that might deter the smugglers from coming into the bay that night.

Chapter 17

A groundsman was painting the wrought iron gates of Woodville House when the barouche drove past, although at that very moment it began to rain and he straightened to leave his task. The barouche halted and Rosamund leaned out.

"Has Miss Davey left yet?"

"Yes, Miss Rosamund. She went with Cluffo Dowdeswell some time ago."

The barouche moved on as the rain fell more heavily, tamping on the roof of the coach. Jessica hoped that Tamsin would have reached the cottage, for she could get very wet in the dogcart. Thunder rumbled across the skies and with it came even heavier rain that was now streaming down in torrents.

They crossed the deserted market square and passed the Feathers where the arched entrance was crowded with people who had been caught by the suddenness of the summer storm. The ford would soon be higher, for the river rose swiftly here, sometimes flooding the inn, although that was usually in more inclement winter weather.

The rain dripped dismally in the trees as they left the town behind. Jessica stared through the trickling rivulets on the window, catching her breath suddenly as she saw a horseman moving through the trees away to her right. She wiped the misty glass and looked out again, in time to see the horse jump a ditch and vanish between the trees toward Ladywood.

Rosamund had seen him, too. "That was Nicholas," she said in surprise. "Whatever is he doing out here at this time?"

"Getting caught in the rain," said Jessica lightly, although inside her heart was sinking. Nicholas was already riding for Ladywood.

Rosamund did not get out of the barouche at Applegarth, and Jessica hurried inside as the carriage turned to make its final journey back to Woodville House. Beneath the dripping roses around the door, Jessica paused, looking toward the crumbling wall where the path vanished into Ladywood. Let it not be that Nicholas was going to watch for the smugglers. Let it be for some other reason that he was out riding tonight.

Tamsin was inside slicing a loaf of whole meal bread. "A fine time the ducks'll have tonight if this keeps up."

"I wondered if you'd get back in time," said Jessica, unbuttoning the pelisse carefully, for it was one of her proudest possessions.

"Oh, I'd no walking to do at all. Cluffo took me

to the farrier, and Jinks and the dogcart was ready and waiting."

"How was Harry Parr?"

"Moaning fit to burst, so I reckon he's all right. Drank a good draught of elderberry wine, anyhow, and had a rosier glow on his cheeks when I left than he had when I arrived."

"I'm not surprised, for I've tasted that devil's brew of yours."

Thunder rolled over the valley again and Jessica shivered. "I'm glad I'm not out in this now."

"There'll be a few damp souls in Ladywood tonight, and serve them right, daft hosebirds. And all for Froggy brandy. It'll do Cluffo's chest no good if'n he's fool enough to go."

Jessica sat down, looking through the window toward the treetops and wondering about Nicholas. "Nicholas is out in this."

"Oh, I knows that. I said to Cluffo that I thought the gentry had more sense but it seemed they didn't."

Jessica felt cold. "You said that to Cluffo? What did you mean?"

"Well, while I was sitting with Harry, Sir Nicholas looked in and said as he'd be riding down by the ruins in Ladywood tonight. He saw me and said as he was helping Sir Francis' keepers. But I knowed that wasn't the truth, but who am I to say so. That was why he was in the wood that night your skirts got caught in the trap, Miss Jess. He were part of the ring. I knows that now, for why else would he be going there tonight?"

"And you told Cluffo he would be in the woods tonight?"

"Yes. Well, why not? It were only in passing and, no doubt, Cluffo knew anyway, seeing as they're in it together."

"Oh, Tamsin, what *have* you done? Cluffo is a smuggler, yes, but Nicholas is a government agent. He's there trying to *catch* them. And you've warned the ring now."

Tamsin put down the bread knife and rubbed her hands anxiously over her apron. "Oh, Miss Jess, tell me you're pulling my leg."

"Would that I was." She looked out at the stormy evening again. It was still light, but only just, for the storm clouds blotted out the last of the sun. "When is the tide in tonight?"

"Ten o'clock, I reckon. Why?"

"And the ring will be there before then to guide in the ship?"

"Happen that's how they does it, I don't rightly know."

"That's about two hours then."

"Two hours for what?"

"To get to the ruins before they do."

"You can't do that. What if they catches you? I can't let you, Miss Jess."

"I can't sit here knowing that he's probably riding into a trap, can I? I must try to warn him. Tamsin, you know what they'll do to him if they catch him."

"There'll be a well-dressed 'natomy floating in the bay at first light."

Jessica stood. "Does the path lead straight to the old abbey?"

"Ah, but you'd be a fool to keep to it. They'll go that way with the donkeys, for it's firm and safe for the animals."

"But I don't know my way through Ladywood."

"You can follow the river. Go down from Applegarth land and pick up the river at the bottom of the woods. It goes right through and passes the ruins before dropping quickly down into the bay beyond. But 'twill be no easy task in this weather, Miss Jess. I'll come with you."

"No. I'll not have you puffing and blowing fit to raise the dead. It will be better on my own."

"Then have a quick sup of the Madeira afore you goes out. It'll warm you up."

As Jessica hurried up the stairs for her old brown mantle, Tamsin poured a liberal cup of wine.

Jessica tied the mantle's floppy hood beneath her chin and drank the wine.

"For the Lord's sake have a care, Miss Jess," pleaded Tamsin anxiously.

The rain swept into the warm kitchen as Jessica opened the front door, and on their hooks above the range the brass pans rattled together in the draft. The air was filled with the sound of the storm and as she stepped out another roll of thunder rippled over the skies. The wet grass dragged against her skirts as she ran toward the gap in the old wall, leaving the telltale path immediately, and following the wall on the boundary of the wood down toward the unseen river. Ivy leaves flapped on the trunks of trees and wound secretly over the roots and stones where she tried to pass.

She picked her way down the boundary slowly, listening for the noise of the river as it babbled over the rocks at the bottom of the valley. The rushing noise passed unnoticed at first in the clamor of rain and thunder, but then she saw the water sweeping around the boulders through a gap in the trees ahead.

The bank was hard and safe as she began to hurry downstream, pushing through the clumps of reeds growing thickly by the water's edge. A startled roe deer that had been drinking from a pool, darted away as Jessica suddenly appeared from beneath the overhanging fronds of a willow tree.

And then she could see the ruins, standing gray and lonely on the level ground above the distant bay, gleaming pearly-white where the sun had broken through the blanket of storm clouds. There, caught in the shaft of bright, late sun, she saw the ship riding at anchor.

Chapter 18

She stood by a rustling alder watching for any sign of movement among the ruins, but all seemed quiet. The clouds closed over the last of the sun, and suddenly she could no longer see the ship in the bay. She brushed aside the leaves to step from the shelter of the bushes by the river's edge. Another growl of thunder sounded almost overhead, but she realized the rain was less heavy now. She could no longer feel the drops striking her shoulders and the moaning of the breeze through the damp wood was louder and clearer. The river slid smoothly past the old abbey, its bed unbroken by boulders, but in the distance she heard it babbling again as it rushed the last mile to the sea.

Slowly she moved on to the level ground by the ruins, pausing as a new scent caught her nostrils. It was a distinctive smell, warm and sweet, and mixed with a trace of leather. There was a horse close by. She froze, her eyes sweeping the tangle of branches and leaves that stretched around the perimeter of the clearing. Then she saw it, a dark shadow by a fallen rowan tree. Even in the eery light of the storm she could see that it was Nicholas' horse, hidden from the abbey by the tree, and safe from approach from the other side because of the river. But where was Nicholas?

She went to the horse to pat its shoulder soothingly. The animal was hot, as if it had only recently been ridden hard. She left the rowan tree and hurried through the thick grass to the nearest ivy-clad wall, flattening against it breathlessly to scan the remainder of the abbey. It was so horribly quiet now, but for the wind over Ladywood. The rain was reduced to wisps of damp gossamer that brushed her skin so delicately she could not feel it. An owl called. The darkness deepened with each passing second.

"Nicholas?" The whisper sounded unnaturally loud.

Something rustled through the grass behind her and with a gasp she turned, her heart thundering as whatever it was came nearer. Then she saw that it was a vixen, her belly close to the ground and her brush dragging behind her as she slunk across the open ground, pausing nervously to look behind as if she heard something. A twig snapped somewhere and the vixen was gone.

Fearfully, Jessica looked in the direction of the sound. The hairs on the nape of her neck prickled with fear and she licked her lips with a tongue

148

that was dry. Stealthy sounds carried on the breeze, as if someone was creeping ever closer to the ruins. Instinct told her she had only just arrived ahead of the smugglers.

"Nicholas?" she whispered again, moving from the shelter of the wall to the next part of the ruin, the remains of a tower where the ground floor rooms were still complete.

"Nicholas, if you are here, for pity's sake answer me!" her voice ended on a sob.

Her heart almost stopped then as a hand closed over her mouth and dragged her into a shadowy doorway. "Jessica, what in God's name are you doing here?" Nicholas shook her, his voice rough with surprise.

She pulled his hand from her mouth urgently. "They know you are here! Tamsin told Cluffo that she heard what you said to Harry Parr. She didn't know what she was doing." She stared from him toward the quiet woods where the stealthy sounds had ceased. "The ship is in the bay already," she whispered, her voice dropping so that he could hardly hear her. "And I heard them coming through the woods a moment ago. They are over that way, cutting off the landward side. There's no escape that way."

"Nor to seaward, for they're already down there, I've been watching. God take Varangian, for I caught no sight of him. I've still no proof of his involvement."

"Why does it matter so much? Let it be, Nicholas, for tonight is the last time anyway."

"It is a matter of the law, Jessica." He looked from the doorway toward the rowan tree. "We could perhaps reach the horse." His arm slipped

149

around her waist. "You should not have come, for this is too dangerous."

"I had to warn you. . . ." She broke off as his arm tightened, drawing her across the open doorway to the other side where he looked at the woods for any sign of danger.

"Well, Jessica, it grieves me to let the ring slip through my fingers, but I value my life above the letter of the law. Below where we stand, in the crypt, is stored so much contraband that I think Varangian must have culled a vast fortune since this all began."

"He needed it," she murmured and he glanced quickly at her. But then a late roll of thunder echoed over Ladywood and a dog began to bark furiously at the sudden sound. It was Nipper.

Nicholas seized the moment, dragging her behind him as he bent low to run across the open ground toward the rowan tree. They reached its shelter and crouched down to listen. Nipper was silenced at last and the stillness returned.

Quickly, Nicholas untethered the horse and mounted, glancing around before reaching down to lift Jessica. As she took his hand the pistol shot rang out and his fingers went limp. She screamed as he slid forward over the horse's shoulders, falling heavily to the ground at her feet. The horse was gone then, its hooves thudding dully on the wet ground as it turned instinctively in the direction of Woodville House. Jessica went to Nicholas, crying out as she saw the slow trickle of blood oozing across his forehead. His eyes were closed and he did not move.

"Oh, Miss Jess, you hadn't ought to have come here."

"Jamie?" She looked up as Jamie bent over to look at the unconscious man.

" 'Tis only a graze, which be a pity as he've got to die now," he said softly, reloading the pistol with slow, steady hands.

"No. No, please, Jamie!" Her hand reached out, trembling.

Beyond him she saw Cluffo, a torch held high. "They'm both dangerous, Jamie, you knows that," muttered the groom anxiously.

Her eyes fled back to Jamie. "Your identities are known anyway," she said quickly. "To kill us would merely add murder to the list of charges against you. Smuggling means deportation, but murder means the gallows."

Jamie nodded. "I know that well enough, but I *don't* know that you're being truthful in this, Jess. By the looks of you I'd say you'd tell me anything to spare his life."

"I would, but it so happens that I am speaking the truth." She met his gaze as squarely as she could, for she must convince him.

"Happen you're an honest woman most of the time, Jess Durleigh, but I've a sight to lose should I choose wrong now."

"You haven't, Jamie. You haven't anything to lose. This was the last run anyway, wasn't it? Well, take everything and go—go to America like you told me you planned."

"And what of him?"

"He can do nothing to stop you."

"He can get the militia on our tails quick as lightning. We'd not make it to Bristol."

"How long do you need?"

"For Bristol? A day."

151

"I can give you a day."

"How?"

"I'll keep him safe for a day, what more can I say?" She glanced at the faces at the edge of the torchlight, but she could not recognize any of them. Was Francis there? Or would he keep from sight?

"Get the line moving," muttered Jamie, jerking his head at Cluffo.

"You ain't going to listen to her, Jamie?"

"Do as I say, or the tide'll turn and we'll miss the last pickings."

"What of me, Jamie? She knows me now."

"Come with me to Bristol or hang."

"You decided to trust her?" Cluffo looked at her with hate in his eyes.

Jamie nodded. "I've no desire to hang for my crimes, my friend. I dursn't risk that our names are known. Woodville ain't no revenue man, he's a government man if ever I saw one. There ain't no more palms to cross with silver now. Get out now and live to fight another day, eh?" Jamie smiled.

"But we're putting us selves in her hands."

"I trust her, Cluffo, and I've good reason to. Haven't I, Jess?"

She nodded.

Cluffo shook his head agitatedly. "But, Dolly! What of her?"

"Dolly wouldn't leave Henbury for a small fortune, you know that. Now get going, Cluffo, or I'll end your botherings here and now." Jamie's pistol moved toward the man's chest.

Cluffo turned away and the small group of men melted away through the ruins toward the beach where a light was flashing on the hidden ship.

In the distance a hound was baying and Jamie glanced toward the sound irritatedly. "Varangian's out again!"

She looked at him. "He's not one of you?"

"Varangian? You must be jesting. He's like a ferret after the poachers every night. He's too honest for my peace of mind is that one."

"Francis has nothing to do with the ring?"

"No."

"Then who is the leader?"

Jamie smiled. "You're talking to him, Jess Durleigh. This ring is mine and mine alone."

"Oh, Jamie, you could have set that brain of yours to something safe and legal, and you could have done so well for yourself."

"Ah, but safe and legal would bore the tail off me. Just like marrying Varangian would have done for you, for I knows you well, Jess."

"And will you leave no sweetheart behind?"

"The only wench I ever had a fancy for have taken to mixing with the nobs. A farmer's daughter, chestnut-haired and with a light in her eye fit to spark an icicle."

She looked steadily at him. "I'm sorry, Jamie."

"There ain't no need. 'Tis nothing I'll pine away over—not Jamie Pike." He smiled. " 'Tis one of the injustices of life that I drags to mind when I've a notion the fire inside me is burning low."

She looked away, brushing the thick gouts of blood from Nicholas' face with the wet cloth of her mantle.

"What have the Woodville's got then, Jess? Tell me that? For first it were that bad lot, Philip, and now this one."

"There's no answer to that question."

"Well, happen you've chosen more wisely this time." He turned to look toward the sea. As he stared, the light on the ship ceased to flash. "It's nearly done now."

Down in the bay a donkey brayed.

"But if Francis is out in Ladywood how will you get through?"

"By going right across Varangian Park, that's how. I'm wise to him now. I know that when he sets out after the poachers he takes all his men with him. Like a dashed army they are. Varangian is daft not guarding his rear. A fine general he'd make, and no mistake."

"Take care, Jamie."

"I shall. Reckon this must be the last time I sees you then, Jess Durleigh."

She stared at him, seeing in him a faint ghost from the past: a tousled-haired boy who had kissed her behind the schoolhouse, and then tugged her hair when she had told her best friend Rosamund.

Through the trees a line of faint lights moved along the shore line and Jamie tucked the pistol into his belt. "It's time I went. A day now, I have your word on it?"

"Yes."

"I'll get him into shelter in the abbey, but that's all I'm doing for you."

"Yes." She stood as he bent to grab Nicholas beneath the arms.

He dragged him slowly across the grass and into the room where earlier, she and Nicholas had stood wondering how to escape. Inside he laid him comfortably on the hard, dry ground.

"He'll be well enough. A mortal bad headache, but no more than that."

"I hope so," she said anxiously, staring at Nicholas' ghastly paleness.

"I knows what I'm talking about. Good-bye then, Jess Durleigh."

"Good-bye, Jamie. And good luck."

He caught her hand and pulled her near, kissing her on the lips. "And don't go telling your best friend this time neither," he murmured, releasing her abruptly. Then he was gone. She heard his footsteps through the long grass before the night swallowed him.

Chapter 19

Nicholas lay so still she thought time and time again that Jamie had been wrong, that he was dead. She cradled his head on her lap, the tears trickling down her cheeks as she pushed her hand inside his shirt to feel the steady beating of his heart.

The men's urgent voices jerked her into alertness again. Through the doorway she could see their silhouettes against the stream.

"Us'll have to swim across here."

"Devil take it, Cob. I can't swim."

"You'll have to, or get catched by Varangian's hounds. Hear 'em?"

The noise of the hounds carried clearly on a gust of wind.

"Drownded or Taunton jail, 'tis a mortal hard choice."

"For you, but not for me. This here be one poacher as isn't going to get his self catched." The taller of the two slid down the bank and into the water. "Come on now, and I'll give a hand. The hounds can't follow our scent over water."

"I'm coming, Cob. Lord help me." The smaller figure followed. "And all for a miserable rabbit I could have catched on the common, and all."

Silently, Jessica watched the two men's heads in the deep, smooth water. She heard one choking and gulping, and then the one called Cob had his friend secure and bore him across the stream to the other side just as Francis' hounds burst from the wood. They were followed by the keepers on horseback and by men on foot carrying torches. Pistol shots ripped the night as the two fugitives scrambled up the opposite bank and vanished into the trees beyond.

Then she realized that the hounds had picked up a new scent. Her arms tightened protectively around Nicholas as the animals began to yelp again and came, tails wagging, toward the room where she knelt. Someone shouted. It was Francis.

"Hold them back, you fools, or they'll tear anyone they catch to pieces."

Someone whistled and the hounds paused almost in the doorway, whining regretfully, but nonetheless obeying the command to return. Francis' horse threw a shadow across the doorway and she saw the pistol he held, rising until it was leveled at the room.

"Come out, or I'll set the dogs on you."

"Francis?" Her voice was small and frightened. The pistol lowered. "Who is that?"

"It's me, Jessica." She was almost weeping again.

158

He dismounted, snapping his fingers for a torch. The wavering flame sent the shadows reeling as he entered, staring in amazement at the strange sight that met his eyes.

"What goes on here? Is Woodville dead?"

"No, just unconscious."

Francis crouched and turned Nicholas' face toward him, nodding. "A bullet scrape, no more. He's been lucky. But who did it?"

She hesitated. She had promised Jamie a day, and a day he would have. "I don't know. I didn't see who did it."

Francis' blue eyes studied her. "Why are you both here on my land in the middle of the night?"

She did not answer.

His eyes lightened. "I can put my own conclusions then? Once a whore always a whore, Jessica?"

Still she said nothing.

He got to his feet. "He'll have to be got to the house and the physician must see that wound." Turning, he called to his men and in a short while Nicholas was being lifted over the back of a horse.

Francis mounted, watching Jessica's anxious face as the horse carrying Nicholas was led slowly away in the direction of Varangian Hall. "You had best ride double with me, Jessica." He held out his hand to her and she took it.

He lifted her lightly before him, his arm steadying her as the horse shifted at the heavier weight. Then, with one final glance across the river where the poachers had made their escape, he waved his arm and the men withdrew.

They moved silently through the dark wood where the wind had risen to make a hissing, whispering sound through the trees, bending the branches and causing the wet leaves to flap. The road above Applegarth was deserted as Francis reined in, turning to a nearby keeper.

"Get into Henbury and rouse the physician. Then go to Woodville House and tell them what has happened."

Jessica touched her arm. "And Applegarth? Tamsin does not know what has happened, either."

He looked at her as if contemplating refusing her, then he nodded. "And tell Miss Davey at the cottage below here, that her mistress is at Varangian Hall and that all is well."

The man kicked his heel and the horse turned, leaping away down the rocky incline, its hoofbeats ratting long after it had passed from sight. A slight sound caught Jessica's ears and she turned sharply, seeing the sudden interest of the hounds whose tails were wagging as they looked into the undergrowth.

"Nipper?" Jessica slipped from Francis' horse and went to the thick, dense covering of bracken.

The puppy crawled out on his belly, whining. He looked up at her with sorrowful eyes. Jessica glanced at the trees beyond the bracken. Was Jamie there? Or had he left Nipper behind?

Francis looked at the puppy. "That's Pike's mongrel. Give him to Chandler."

She picked up Nipper and handed his wet little body to the man who urged his horse closer. The puppy whined again and struggled slightly, but seemed disinclined to make much of an effort.

Francis helped her onto his horse again and the party moved more quickly now along the

160

road toward the great gates of Varangian Hall. A few lights blazed from the windows, reflecting on the ornamental lake where the boats were drawn up onto the grass. There were no pretty colored lanterns now, no lights illuminating the fountains and statues, and Jessica's heart was heavy. She sat quietly on the horse as Francis dismounted, watching the men carefully lift Nicholas' body and carry him into the house.

Francis reached up to help her dismount. "The physician will not be long," he muttered, as if reluctant to say anything comforting.

"Please, Francis, do not persist in being so unkind to me, for I do not deserve it. I have done nothing for which you should blame me." The shock of all that had happened brought tears to her eyes again, and she knew that if he said one cruel word now she would cry.

He began to walk into the house. "You had best come in, for I believe there is much we should say. To clear matters up, if nothing else." He walked inside, the chandeliers of the black-and-white tiled entrance hall burnished his golden hair, and he waited as she followed him, a bedraggled little figure with muddy feet, soaking-wet mantle, and hair that clung in rats' tails around her pale face.

" 'Pon my soul," he said sarcastically, "what would the drawing-room biddies have to say could they see you now? The notorious Miss Durleigh, a sight to be spoken of with great relish by those less well-endowed than herself."

She said nothing, staring at the muddy footprints she had left behind on the polished tiles.

He seemed unable to control his dislike. "I was

prepared to be kind to you on your return, Jessica. To welcome you back to Henbury and prove to the world that you were not as had been said."

She looked up at the impassive faces of the footmen standing at the foot of the red-carpeted stairs to the ballroom. "If you must talk to me like this, pray choose a more private place, Francis."

He walked to some large gold and white doors and threw them open. "We may shout at each other in complete privacy in here," he said, standing aside as she walked slowly past him into the drawing room.

"I will not shout at you, Francis," she said wearily as he closed the door.

"You were Philip Woodville's mistress, and I believe you were also his accomplice."

"No."

"Then how. . . ."

"I told you, it was the stolen mail bag."

"Maybe so, but there is still the matter of the note."

"Note?" She remembered what Rosamund had confided in her.

"Yes. Oh, come now, Jessica. Let's not play games over this. You know what note as well as I do."

"No, I don't."

He took off his mantle and threw it across the back of a chair. "The gambling note of my father's."

She stared, shaking her head.

He poured himself some cognac, pausing a moment before pouring a second and handing it to her. "Everyone knew he gambled heavily, and drank with equal excess."

"It was no secret. But he died five years ago."

"Before he died he gambled Varangian Hall away. He lost at *vingt-et-un,* to a man called O'Connor—a drunken little Irishman who was arrested the same night for stealing from Woodville House."

"And?"

"Only three men in the world knew about the high stakes that were played and lost at that game. My father, O'Connor, and Philip Woodville, my father's *alter ego* in vice and sin. O'Connor was in poor health, a bronchial condition that worsened with each month spent languishing in Taunton jail. My father lived in anguish, waiting for O'Connor to make some move to reclaim what was now rightfully his, and in the end he killed himself rather than face the ruin. He told no one what had happened, hoping against hope, I suppose, that the truth would never come out, for O'Connor was, of a certainty, a long time silent. But O'Connor was himself close to death. He died within a week of my father, and Philip Woodville took himself along to Taunton to reclaim the dead man's belongings, 'to send to his widowed mother in Dublin.' He got his hands on the note, and so it all began—the blackmail and torment that have been my lot since inheriting all this." He waved his arm to encompass the house.

"So it is not yours?"

He shrugged. "I know not who else it belongs to. O'Connor had no relatives and left no will. But, no doubt, the would-be heirs would come flocking were the tale to become common knowledge."

"Oh, Francis, I swear to you I knew nothing of

163

this. Philip said nothing to me, and indeed I had no idea that he was anything other than the sweet, gentle man I loved. Please believe me, for you must know I would never hurt you."

He looked at her for a long while. "If it is not you who has the note, then who is it? Someone must have it, for it did not come to light after Philip's death. It must still be in existence, and while it is, I am not secure here."

"Then do you believe me?"

He put down his glass and took her hand, nodding. "I believe you. Fear and uncertainty make monsters of men like me. Forgive me."

"Francis, if there have been no demands, except that one from the stolen bag, then it must be that whoever has the note does not intend using it. Perhaps it could be even that Philip destroyed it."

"That I know not to be so. He would have destroyed his passport to a small and steady fortune for life? Why should he? No, it still exists, and someone has it. Jessica, I *must* have it. Varangian Hall belongs to me, to my family, to my heirs when I marry. I want Rosamund to be mistress of all this, and yet I cannot take her for my wife until all this is ended. Do you understand that, for I fear Rosamund does not."

"I understand *you* and I understand her. She wants to be with you wherever and however you are. You, on the other hand, are so much the gentleman, wanting to come to her with all this to offer." Jessica turned as hoofbeats sounded along the driveway. Drawing aside the net drapes she saw the man Chandler and the physician.

"The physician. . . ." She almost ran to the door, but Francis stopped her.

"No, you cannot go, it would not be decorous."

"But I have no reputation left to protect."

"Then now is as good a time as any to begin. It's only a small head wound, he'll recover quickly."

Jessica sat down, her back straight, her hands folded in her lap. She heard the butler take the physician up the stairs.

Francis poured himself another glass of cognac. "Why were you and Woodville in Ladywood? And how did he get shot?"

"I cannot say."

"Cannot? Or will not? The latter, I suspect."

"Francis, you of all men should understand, for I gave my word to a friend."

"A greater friend than Woodville?"

"An older friend."

His blue eyes rested on her. "A mongrel-owning friend, perchance?"

She said nothing, but she knew her cheeks had reddened.

"Young Pike never goes anywhere without his hound, and yet tonight we find that atrocious Nipper all alone." He swirled the cognac in his glass. "I fancy that I shall have to get my illicit French brandy elsewhere from now on."

"You were on the list?"

"Occasionally. For the occasional blind eye. I suspected Pike was involved. He was, by far, too quick and clever, his mind darting in all directions at once and leaving me standing. He had to be more than a mere shepherd—he could not

165

have been content otherwise. But Woodville is another matter. Was he? . . ."

"No. Nicholas was trying to catch them."

"And so where do you stand? With Nicholas or with Jamie?"

"It is not a question of that. Jamie has gone now. There'll be no more smuggling through Ladywood. All he asks is a day's start. I gave him my word."

"And Nicholas?"

"No. He does not know. He was shot before I saw Jamie. Jamie could have killed us both, but he did not. I have confided this in you, Francis. *Please* honor the confidence."

"My dear, Jessica, who am I to pass comment upon anyone else's conduct? Besides, anyone who knocks Nicholas Woodville down to size cannot be wholly bad."

"You don't like him?"

"He has made his dislike for me somewhat noticeable, and I cannot pretend not to have noticed. There is only one likeable Woodville, and she is that only by marriage."

"Rosamund?"

He nodded. "I love her, Jessica. I love her very much."

"She is leaving Woodville House to come to me. Did you know?"

"No. She should not."

"Lady Amelia has danced a merry jig over her being seen with you so soon after Philip's death. Rosamund asked me to give her shelter and I agreed."

"We are in your debt, it would seem."

"Not really."

He saw the nervous twisting of her hands. "And what does Nicholas say?"

"He doesn't know yet."

"I doubt that he'll approve."

"I know."

"And still you would do it?"

"How could I refuse her? I could not condemn her to Lady Amelia's care merely because I think Nicholas might not approve. Even if I were certain of his disapproval, I could not refuse her, for no one should have to endure that old dragon."

"She has a certain way with her, I will admit. The more so since her precious Philip died. Forgive me, Jessica, but I cannot and will not speak gently of him."

"I understand. You know, he could be so charming and gentle, so very good to be with. It is so sad he was all these other things, too. I wish he had never left me Applegarth, for then I would never have known the truth."

"If you would consider for a moment; he made certain of your eventual disillusionment, for he insisted you come here for a period of two years if you wished to have the cottage. He knew you would have no choice but to return to Henbury. That was the nature of the man—perverse and unkind. In the end, always unkind, even to you."

"But would I have known? Until the stolen mail bag came to light, you had said nothing to me and I doubt that you would ever have, were you not so pushed beyond endurance by the thought of it all beginning again. I would have known that he was not liked, but no more than that."

Francis stared at the cognac. "Unless he was

sure that in the event of his death, not only would you come back to Henbury, but the note would be in someone's hands who would know how to use it."

"I think we romance a little now, don't you? It is a little farfetched to think of Philip planning so much for something to happen after his death, when he was in perfect health and still a young man? He was not to know he was to catch a dangerous malady that would take him so quickly."

"Perhaps you are right. I am so consumed with loathing for the man, I consider him capable of anything. The physician is coming." He stood as someone knocked on the gold and white doors.

"Enter."

"Sir Francis?" The physician's eyes slid to Jessica's bedraggled figure and back to Francis. "I have dressed the wound and cleansed it. Sir Nicholas is still unconscious and likely to remain so for some time. How did it happen?"

"No one appears to quite know. No doubt, he will tell us himself when he regains consciousness."

"Yes, quite so. I'll take myself back to my bed then." The physician glanced at Jessica again. "I'll send my account, Sir Francis."

Francis nodded.

When the man had gone, Jessica stood. "I shall go to him now, Francis," she announced determinedly.

He smiled suddenly.

"What is so amusing?"

"I was thinking of Lady Amelia having to endure Rosamund and myself, and then Nicholas and you. She'll have a fit of the vapors that will

168

lay Henbury by the ears. And I'll warrant she'll do all in her power to prevent both matches."

"There is a match for you and Rosamund. But Nicholas has said nothing to me of such a thing. He will not consider marrying his brother's mistress—my own common sense tells me as much." She lowered her eyes unhappily.

"If he loves you, he will marry you regardless. I would be unjust to him were I to state otherwise. He is not one to abide by the endless stream of do's and don'ts society insists upon ranging before us all. He is in the second room beyond my study upstairs. I will send a maid in a short while to take you to your own room. With some luck to smile on you, you may sleep for what remains of the night. Oh, and I shall send one of my dressing robes for you."

She smiled, closing the door behind her.

Chapter 20

The morning brought Rosamund in the Woodville barouche. Holding her breath Jessica peeked from the curtains of Nicholas' rooms, but there was no sign of Lady Amelia.

She turned to look at Nicholas. He had wakened briefly during the night. His head was bandaged and he lay so still that each time she looked she feared his heart had ceased to beat. It was a foolish notion that insistently forced its way into her head and could only be calmed by sitting beside him, holding his hand and feeling the pulse in his wrist. She sat there now, looking across the rolling parkland toward the sunlit bay. There was no trace of the storm now and the rain had washed everything until it was clear and sparkling. Even the trees seemed a fresher green.

Where was Jamie Pike now? Had he and Cluffo reached Bristol?

Rosamund came in, her delicate pink skirts rustling slightly. "Jess? How is he?"

"He is still not awake."

"Francis says it is nothing to worry about."

"I know."

"But still you worry."

"Yes."

"Jess, did you speak to him about Francis?" Rosamund stood the other side of the blue and white bed. "Or about me coming to Applegarth?"

"No. There was no time before the accident."

"Francis told me. It's Jamie isn't it?"

"How? . . ."

"It was not difficult for me to worm the story from Francis. Why are you protecting Jamie?"

"He spared our lives."

"He's crafty enough to know not to add murder to his name. I doubt if he'd have shot you anyway."

"It does not matter now. But I wanted to help him. Surely you would do the same?"

"I do not think my memories of Jamie Pike and the old schoolyard are as tender as yours, for I associate those days with the sudden deterioration in my family's fortune, the loss of my comfortable tutor, and my initiation into the horrible farmyard ways of country children—yourself included, Jessica. You were the most awful terror when first I knew you. You and Jamie, together, made my life a misery until you decided I was perhaps not so bad after all. After that I enjoyed things, but Jamie pinched and poked me when-

172

ever the chance presented itself, for he lost you to me and he did not like it."

"Jamie was all right. He could have done worse had he wished."

"And now you are protecting him." Rosamund's eyes were thoughtful.

"Don't look like that. Just leave the matter alone for all your guesses would be wrong."

"Well, you are going to have to endure Nicholas' suspicions on the same point, for he is certain to wonder when he knows."

"There is no need for him ever to know. Is there, Rosamund? You and Francis must hold your chattering, and all will be well."

"You aren't going to identify Jamie?"

"No."

"The scoundrel does not deserve it."

"Maybe not. But, Rosamund, if you persist in this, I swear I shall quarrel with you." Jessica stood agitatedly. There was nothing to be read in her actions, yet somehow it seemed she was going to be misunderstood. She looked at Rosamund suddenly. "How are you out of Lady Amelia's clutches again?"

"I told her I was going to Miss Brendon's haberdashery. My baggage has been packed though, and is in the boot of the barouche. I am not going back there, Jessica. I am taking you at your word about Applegarth."

"My word is good." Jessica looked at Nicholas. Would he understand? Would he forgive her interference in his family's affairs?

Rosamund straightened the coverlet and tucked in Nicholas' limp hand. "I was not going to come

173

here at all this morning, but I know that Lady Amelia intends driving over in the landau before noon. I guessed you would still be here, so I came to warn you. You and I should leave now and go to Applegarth immediately."

Jessica nodded.

Rosamund went to the door. "Well, come on then. Don't stand there daydreaming, or she will come and catch us both and I could not bear a confrontation."

"I was just thinking about Jamie. He was part of my childhood—I had a very happy childhood—part of my life, really. Henbury will not be the same without him." She bent to kiss Nicholas on the cheek, running her fingers across his lips gently, then she followed Rosamund from the room.

As the door closed on the two women, Nicholas' eyes opened. He stared at the window toward the shimmering sea. "Am I to compete with a shepherd then, Jessica? I think not."

The barouche drove smartly down the hillside, with Jessica holding a bag containing her soiled clothes, and leaning from the window all the time, fearing to see the elegant landau approaching from the opposite direction.

They had alighted at Applegarth and the barouche had been sent back to Woodville House, when they heard the other carriage. From the drawing room window they watched its slow progress up the incline. Inside, Lady Amelia sat bolt upright, her hands resting on her pearl-handled cane, her face directed proudly frontwards. Not by so much as a flicker did she appear even to notice the cottage.

Rosamund sat on the settle, swallowing. "Well, it is done now, Jess. There's no going back to the old harridan now."

Tamsin looked at the girl's tense face. "Well, I reckons as how a nice cup of good Pekoe wouldn't go amiss. Miss Jess?"

"Yes, Tamsin. That is an excellent idea."

"How be Sir Nicholas then?"

"He came round once during the night, but he was still asleep when we left."

"He'll have a head like a bucket and all, poor man. I knows!"

Jessica watched her placing the old kettle on the range. "The man Chandler brought the message that I was all right?"

"Oh, aye. He came not long after Jamie were here."

"Jamie?"

"Aye. He had that there pup with him. Said he was leaving Henbury and how he wanted you to have the pup. Said there weren't no one else he'd rather had him."

Jessica blushed, feeling Rosamund's curious gaze. "I don't even like the animal."

"Well, it don't rightly matter now, for not a moment after Jamie'd gone, riding like some 'at possessed on that there horse he do seem to have got from somewhere, the puppy upped and went. Leapt straight out of my arms he did, and followed the horse. At least he went the way he thought the horse had gone, but actually he went the way it had come from in the first place. Back up toward Varangian."

"Sir Francis has him now. I suppose I must ask for him back if I am his new owner."

"He be a nice little varmint. A might yapp'' but then he's only a pup. Living here we ought to have a guard dog, and I reckon that there Nipper be the best I've heard in a twelve month or more." Tamsin poured the boiling water into the teapot, and Rosamund looked away from the gleaming silver a little uncomfortably as she recalled the last time she had seen it—and the use to which she had put it.

The cups and saucers rattled as Tamsin set them on the table. "There be a strange thing, too. Dolly Dowdeswell's brother were here first thing. It seems that Jamie and Cluffo have upped and gone together. A strange mixing that be and all. Still, Cluffo drank all his money, so I doubt that Dolly'll notice the difference, 'cepting there'll be less washing and less food to find. Good for nothing, were Cluffo."

Rosamund smiled. "Not like the inestimable Harry Parr?"

Tamsin went a fiery red. "I don't know what you means, Miss Rosamund."

"Really? Well, Sir Nicholas told me once how glowingly Mr. Parr spoke of you. And I could not help but notice how concerned you were about his health."

"Such nonsense. He be family, no more and no less." But Tamsin looked pleased. "Spoke well of me, did he? Well, I never."

Chapter 21

Jessica sat on the grassy bank above the cottage, gazing unhappily at the spire of St. Mary's nestling in the valley away to her left. It was a week now since Nicholas had been shot. He had left Varangian Hall three days later, driving alone in the barouche past Applegarth. She had seen him. He had not stopped to see her. He had not even glanced at the entrance as the barouche swung toward Henbury.

She picked a blade of grass and drew her finger along it. Why? Why not even a word? She could not go to visit him, to inquire after him—especially since the whole of Henbury was buzzing with the news of Rosamund's flight from Woodville House.

She watched Jinks pulling the little dogcart away up the incline behind her, and raised her hand to wave to Rosamund and Tamsin. Rosamund was visiting Francis again, and Tamsin would not hear of her going without a chaperon, "to make certain as there was no talk." Rosamund looked radiant, living in so happy a haze now that she hardly noticed how quiet and withdrawn Jessica had become. And if Tamsin noticed, she kept her observations to herself. Jessica moved to sit more comfortably and heard the rustling of paper in her reticule as she set it more firmly on the bank beside her. Inside was the letter from Mr. Slade of Bath. She had quite forgotten the jeweler's little book, but he evidently had remembered where he had left it and now wanted it returned.

A horse moved slowly along the road from Henbury and she hardly noticed it at first. Then she sat up, for there was no mistaking that it was Nicholas. Down by the cottage Nipper began to bark, rushing backward and forward like something demented as the horse turned into the cottage grounds.

She stood up, brushing down her cream-colored skirts. Her heart was thundering as she descended the bank, but she knew immediately something was wrong, for he did not dismount but waited for her to come to the horse's side.

"Miss Durleigh." He inclined his head politely.

"Sir Nicholas." It was like addressing a stranger. His dark eyes were cool and he did not smile. And he called her Miss Durleigh.

He glanced at Nipper who still capered noisily around the horse's legs. "Are you not going to control that beast for a moment, that we may speak?"

"Nipper!" Jessica scooped the excited puppy into

178

the cottage and closed the door. "Yes, Sir Nicholas, and how may I help you?" She was glad her voice sounded detached.

"I am assured you must have spoken with the smugglers in Ladywood on the night I was shot."

"Indeed?"

He nodded. "With one Jamie Pike, late of this parish."

"I spoke with Jamie, yes." Inside the cottage Nipper continued his noise, an audible reminder of Jamie.

"And what did he say?"

"That he was the leader of the ring. He made no attempt at concealing the fact."

"And you suppressed this information."

"I did not. I assumed I would see you shortly afterward, but that was obviously not to be. You have asked and I have immediately told you."

"And yet you were found not an hour after the incident, and said nothing. And so Pike and his friends escaped without capture. You have much to answer for, Miss Durleigh."

How did he know all this? She stared at him, swallowing. Had Francis told him? She immediately set aside that possibility, for although Francis might tell Rosamund, he would not have confided in Nicholas. She decided to attack, as that appeared to be Nicholas' ploy. "And when did you become aware of this?"

"The following day."

"And yet waited until now before coming to ascertain if the information was correct? How remiss of you, Sir Nicholas."

"It was remiss of me not to pay more heed to the convictions of others concerning you, Miss

· Durleigh. Not only content with eloping with my brother, you now return to lure poor, foolish Rosamund into your immoral ways. He glanced at the yellow door where the furious Nipper was scratching. "I wonder you did not consider concealing Pike here, for how charmingly apt that would have been. I trust he left you only his dog to remember him by."

She stepped back. "Good day, Sir Nicholas," she said in a husky voice, turning on her heel to open the kitchen door.

As she went in the delighted Nipper exploded out, to caper around the nervous horse again. Inside she leaned against the door, tears streaming down her face. She heard the horse canter away, followed by Nipper as far as the cottage boundary, where the puppy contented himself with sending abusive barks down the lane in Nicholas' wake.

She went to sit in the quiet drawing room, staring at the pane of glass that had been broken by Rosamund and now was boarded over until the glazier could come. It seemed everything was set on going wrong. Somehow, Nicholas believed she and Jamie had been lovers. And that, together with her support for Rosamund, had turned him from her so completely, it was almost as if he had never been gently inclined toward her at all.

"This won't do, Jessica Durleigh," she told herself sternly, getting to her feet and wiping her face. No, it wouldn't do at all. Sitting, moping about a man as stubborn and easily persuaded aginst her as Nicholas Woodville. She brought a light mantle from her room and went out, followed by Nipper who walked quietly at her feet. She automatically crossed the footpath and entered Ladywood, preferring the soft, green coolness of the woods to the open and sunny hill behind the cottage.

She walked without paying much heed to the direction she took. With something of a jolt, therefore, she found herself standing at the edge of the clearing by the abbey. There was no contraband in the crypt now, for the revenue men had cleared it completely. There would be no more lines of donkeys and men moving silently through the dark hours from ships anchored in the bay. Nipper suddenly whined, staring toward the ruins, his whole body quivering.

"What is it?" she asked, bending to pat the puppy.

He bounded forward, dashing across the open ground to the room where she had knelt with Nicholas. Hesitatingly, she followed him, listening carefully. But he did not bark, he was whining still, although she could not see him. In the doorway she halted, unable to see in the darkness after the bright sun outside. But she recognized his voice as he spoke to the puppy.

"Jamie? Jamie, is it really you?"

Then she could see him as he smiled at her. "Yes, Miss Durleigh, 'tis the bad coin come back again."

"But why? I thought you'd be safe on the way to America by now."

"High tide tonight, that's when I goes. I lost time—my horse was lame. Cluffo got into Bristol afore me and got caught, and to save himself he spilt my name. I just got out with my neck. I sent a message in with a friend, and it was arranged with a merchantman bound for New York that he'd be off Varangian Bay tonight at high tide. So, here I wait. At least I know they'll not think to look for me here."

"Oh, Jamie, I thought you were safe now."

"You've been crying, haven't you? What's gone wrong for you?" He held out his hand and she took it, sitting beside him on the hard floor.

"Just about everything."

"That Nicholas been playing you bad then?"

"He thinks he's justified. Jamie, do you know, he thinks that I was your lover and that was why I said nothing about you being here that night."

"Would that he were right and all!" He grinned, squeezing her hand.

"You would—Tamsin says you're a hosebird and she's right."

"I've never denied it. Bad through and through, that's Jamie Pike." His smile faded. "But he've upset you good and proper, haven't he? Damn nobs, they're all the same when it comes down. Selfish, arrogant, thoughtless, and stupid. Do he really imagine you'd bed with the likes of me?"

"Jamie!"

"Bed be what we're on about, even if you don't like to say so."

"I know."

"Well, if 'tis done, 'tis done. Let him think it, Jess. He ain't worth your tears if'n he's so mulish." He sniffed and rubbed his leg, pushing the delighted Nipper away. "Jess, if'n I went with you back as far as the boundary wall, d'you reckon as how you could give me a bite to eat? I'm that hungry I could eat Nipper here."

182

"Of course." She stood. "I should go back anyway, or Tamsin will be back and wondering where I am."

They walked slowly back through the woods, Jessica gradually falling back into her quiet mood. A pox on Nicholas Woodville, she thought miserably, for she knew she still loved him. Jamie watched her, and as she hurried into the cottage for some bread and cheese and some of Tamsin's elderberry wine for him, he knew that the solution of her problems lay with him, if he dared to do what he should. When she returned, he kissed her cheek gently, smiling at her.

"You're a treasure, Jess Durleigh, and *I* knows that, anyway."

"Make sure you catch that merchantman tonight, Jamie."

"I will."

She went back to the cottage and he melted into Ladywood as the dogcart appeared on the slope from Varangian Hall.

Munching the bread and cheese, he returned to the ruins, pausing only by the rowan tree where his horse was tethered. He slapped its shoulder thoughtfully. Then he sat on the bank to drink the elderberry wine.

"Well, Sir Nicholas High and Mighty Woodville, it do look as if you and me have got to have a little talk, and there ain't no time like the present." He threw the wine bottle into the river where it bobbed away like a boat, then he mounted and turned the horse into Ladywood.

Chapter 22

Henbury Lake was quiet in the early evening sun, and the air was gentle with the lapping of the water around the little jetty. Jamie halted his horse at the water's edge and looked at Nicholas who lounged in one of the boats staring thoughtfully across the dappled, dancing waters.

"You be a hard man to find, Sir Nicholas Woodville." Jamie spoke softly, leveling his pistol toward the startled man.

"Pike!"

"Ah. Pike. *Mr.* Pike while I holds this here pistol."

Nicholas smiled faintly, sitting up and flicking some dust from his cream-colored breeches. "And what brings you back to this neighborhood? Or perhaps I already know the answer to that."

"You'm wrong about Jess Durleigh."

"Jess? You would appear to be on rather intimate terms with the lady, for me to doubt what I suspect."

"Ah, I calls her Jess. And why not? I knowed her when we was children together. My father were only a shepherd—he was Sir Francis' father's head man—and he reckoned as how an education would do me no harm and perhaps a lot of good. So, Jamie Pike went to school and sat alongside Farmer Durleigh's daughter, and alongside Miss Rosamund. Reckon I didn't learn that much, but I learned then to call a pretty green-eyed girl by her first name, and growing up don't seem to change that."

Nicholas yawned. "Spare me your life story, man, and come to the point of all this."

"That be the point. She and me we grew up together. She's a friend, a *good* friend, the sort that don't come by that often in life. She stands by you, and this time it've cost her dear. I don't like that, Sir Nicholas Woodville. You think as how I've been enjoying her favors, don't you?"

"How quaintly expressive a turn of phrase. Yes, I believe that."

"Then you don't merit nothing of her. She loves you, God help her, and she wouldn't lie alongside of me. In Henbury you don't go with your brother, and that's all I be to her—her brother. I may be only on the level of an insect in your eyes, Sir Nob Woodville, but to her I'm as good as anyone, and I'd fight Old Bogey his self to help her. Jess Durleigh have never treated me as anything but her brother—and if I'd thought there was a chance I'd have had her years ago and no mistake. Because, Sir Nob, I do look at her and it be no sister

I sees. She's yours, if'n you'd the sense you was, no doubt, born with. But you being so blue-blooded, likely you don't know a good thing when you sees it."

"Likely," replied Nicholas, looking shrewdly at the horseman. "You must love her very much to come out of hiding like this on her account."

"Even insects have feelings like loving, and conscience, and a sense of what's right and wrong—mostly what's right and wrong, that is."

"Indeed."

"Well, now you knows the truth on it. Jess haven't done nothing she shouldn't with me. What you does now is up to you."

"Am I to thank you for this lecture on life?"

Jamie pushed his pistol into his belt. "You ought to. Ah, you ought to, right enough, but I reckon as you won't."

"And what do you intend to do with me now, Pike? Send me to the bottom of the lake with all flags flying? Or, as our American friends would say, hog-tie me and deposit me at the door of Applegarth?"

"No, Sir Nob. You'd be no use to her at the bottom of Henbury Lake. And if you're going to Applegarth then you goes by your own power—that'd be only right. And if you crawled on your belly that'd be even more right, for you've done her wrong in this, Sir Nob."

"So, I am to survive intact. How then do you propose keeping me silent concerning your presence here?"

"Oh, that be easy. Just stand slow like and come ashore. That's right, nice and smooth, so's my finger don't get too itchy. Now then, Sir Nob

Woodville, you just walk along that path over there, still nice and slow, for I reckon you knows how good a shot I am."

Nicholas walked up the path that wound up the slope from the lake side. The ground was covered with bracken and small, silver birches, and the path was almost overgrown, so rarely was it used. They came into a small clearing where a ramshackle hut stood. It was used to store hurdles, and was damp and cool inside, for the hut stood beneath an oak tree whose spreading branches held off the sun and kept the ground moist even in summertime.

"My prison, I take it," asked Nicholas.

"That's right. Nice and lonely, it be, too. I reckon by the time you gets out of here, I shall be long gone, and safe to boot."

"I'll grant you the point, Pike. But my horse has surely not offended you, so pray set it loose that it will return to the stable at Woodville House."

"Oh, no, I'm not that foolish neither. A riderless horse would have half the town out looking for you and that don't suit my orders. I'll take your horse, though, and it'll be returned to you safe and sound. And if you're not seen around in three days' time, then you'll be set free."

"I trust my ingenuity will have got me out rather sooner than that."

"Happen it'll give you something to think about. Inside now." Jamie drew the pistol again.

He stepped into the hut, brushing a cobweb that dragged across his face and clung stickily. He turned as Jamie dismounted and pushed the door to, lowering the heavy bar across.

Jamie mounted, maneuvering his horse close to the door. "Think on what you've been told, Sir Nob. If you don't love her and don't want her, that be one thing. But if you do and you thought I'd been lapping the cream first, that be quite another."

"Thank you, Mr. Pike. And believe me, I say that from the bottom of my heart."

Surprised, Jamie sat back in the saddle staring at the door. "Reckon nobs might have some sense after all," he muttered, turning his horse to go back down the bracken path to the lake. There he took the reins of Nicholas' horse and rode back across the fields skirting the town and moving swiftly down the steep lane to Cob Darnwell's small cottage. Cob would see all was well with Sir Nob Woodville *and* his horse.

Tamsin drove poor old Jinks at a spanking pace all the way from Henbury, the dogcart sending up clouds of dust that marked her progress through the lanes. She halted the tired pony outside Applegarth and pushed open the door where Jessica and Rosamund stared at her in amazement.

"Tamsin? Whatever is it?" Jessica stood, startled.

"It be Sir Nicholas, Miss Jess. He'm vanished, like a puff of smoke. Early today he were seen on the road to Henbury Lake, but since then not a sign's been seen. They'm out looking now."

"But he's a grown man, and if he sees fit to stay out, then surely. . . ."

"Ah, but he had an important appointment with the magistrate in Henbury at five o'clock, and he

189

didn't keep it, and that don't be like Sir Nicholas. A stickler, is that one."

"But why all the fuss? And you've driven poor Jinks nearly into the ground. Look at him out there, poor thing."

"Well, I just thought ... I just thought that maybe you'd like to know, seeing as how you're in love with him."

"I will correct you there, Tamsin, for I have no wish to know anything at all concerning Sir Nicholas. Not anymore."

"On account of he've not been out here?"

"That. And other things."

"Well, that be up to you."

"That's right."

Rosamund looked at Jessica. "I have been so wrapped up in my own happiness that I have not seen how unhappy you are, Jess. I'm sorry for my thoughtlessness."

"It's no fault of yours, Rosamund. Besides, it is all over and done with now."

"I don't believe that."

"And neither do I," said Tamsin, untying her bonnet.

Jessica sat down and picked up her embroidery again. "And how are matters with you and Francis now?" she asked, defying either woman to pursue the matter of Nicholas Woodville.

Tamsin sighed heavily and went out to unharness the pony. Rosamund took the novel she had been reading and closed it. "We went to see the vicar of St. Mary's today. He will not marry us. Lady Amelia has seen to that. The Woodville family have been patrons of the church for centu-

190

ries, it seems, and he will not risk losing them to St. Jude's over in Rendlecombe. She was there, standing at Philip's grave. She was smiling a little and we knew that she guessed how our interview with the vicar had gone. Oh, I hate that woman. I hate her more than I ever thought possible. She tries to keep Philip alive, you know. She wants me to behave like a sweet, swooning widow for the rest of my life, and for his good name to be perpetuated. Good name! The man was so wicked, I suspect even the doors of Hell hesitated before letting him in."

"Rosamund! Don't say that, for I knew him only as good."

"He was evil."

"Surely not, for I swear if he were that bad even I would have noticed. You exaggerate because you hated him."

Rosamund ran her fingers over the spine of the book. "Did you know that she won't let anyone into his room at the big house? Each night she goes in before retiring and turns backs the coverlets as if he were going to sleep there that night. She even lights the oil lamp and leaves it burning; replenishing the oil when it runs low, and trimming the wick. It's so very horrible. It's obscene. And then she sits in that churchyard staring at his tomb, putting fresh flowers there and kneeling, herself, to draw out any weeds that have the audacity to flourish. There is something very wrong with such behavior."

Jessica shuddered. "She loved him. She cannot help how she behaves now."

"She's like a great, loathsome spider sitting in

191

the middle of a web, watching everything and planning how to strike down the next unfortunate fly."

"I will agree to that description."

Tamsin came in and went to make a pot of tea. "Cob Danwell will be here shortly. I saw him in Henbury and he said as how at high tide, him and some others be going to the bay to raise the lobster pots. Should be a good catch. I told him as how we'd like one—for allowing him and his poaching cronies to use Applegarth to come and go by."

"And he agreed?"

"Oh, aye, and why not? Nice bit of lobster'd go down a treat, I reckon. Shouldn't be long now. 'Twas high tide half an hour since."

Jessica looked in the direction of the sea. Had Jamie caught the merchantman?

Tamsin went to the shelf to take down the tea caddy and exclaimed with annoyance. "There! I went and forgot that there Mr. Slade's book after all. 'Tis still here, all neatly packed and sealing-waxed, and I've been and come back."

"I'll take it tomorrow," said Rosamund, "for Francis is taking me into Henbury on the way to Padbury."

"Padbury?"

"The Varangian family have been patrons of Padbury Church for years, so we must go there if we hope to be married."

"And Francis says no more about his troubles?"

"I think, at last, he knows that I want him no matter what his circumstances are. Anyway, he has said no more about it, but I can tell how

192

worried he is, all the same. He won't tell me anything."

"Perhaps it is not as serious as you imagine," said Jessica, hoping she sounded convincing.

"Perhaps." Rosamund sighed, opening her book again.

Chapter 23

Jessica sat writing a list for Tamsin to take to Miss Brendon's haberdashery. "Do you think yellow ribbon, or cream for the sprigged muslin gown?"

"Don't rightly know, Miss Jess. Happen yellow, though."

"Yellow it is. And some of that Brussels lace I saw in her window last week."

"I wonder if they've found Sir Nicholas yet."

"He only went missing yesterday afternoon. I still think it foolish to send out searchers like that. Perhaps he has a mistress he chose to visit."

"Do you believe that?"

"I would believe anything of Sir Nicholas Woodville, Tamsin. Anything at all. There, that is the list complete. And tell her I won't have any lace if it's at the end of the bolt, for she's tried that before and I've found the pin marks."

"Right. I'll not be long, Miss Jess. Though, on reflection, perhaps I'll go on the wagonette, for 'tis market day. I wants to see Dolly Dowdeswell, for I hear as how Cluffo was caught up Bristol way. Jamie Pike got away, though. That young hosebird do have a charmed life, I reckon. Would you mind if'n I visited her?"

"Of course not. By the way, how is Harry Parr now?"

"Happen he's well enough. The great curmudgeon, he sent me a bunch of roses from his garden."

"That great curmudgeon could have done nothing at all, and would that have pleased you?"

"No, reckon not. He'm a good man, is Harry."

"And he obviously thinks you're not so bad either." Jessica smiled at Tamsin's pink face. "Listen, there is the wagonette now."

"I'll be back on it sometime this afternoon then."

"Good-bye."

"Good-bye, Miss Jess."

Jessica watched Tamsin hurry out to wave down the wagonette. When it had gone she turned and her glance fell upon Mr. Slade's book again. She sighed. Rosamund had forgotten it, and now Tamsin had gone, too, and the cursed book still remained firmly upon her shelf.

Out in the orchard Nipper began to bark. He was tied by a long piece of rope to a tree trunk, for Tamsin had bought some chickens that were in a small run next to the stables. She had tied the cross puppy to keep him from worrying the birds—"And there you'm going to stay, young Nipper, lessen you scares my fowls. And when you shows as you can behave yourself like a proper young gentleman, then you can come off the rope, but not until then."

Jessica looked from the window to where the agitated pup was straining and jumping, and she saw the reason for his clamor. The Woodville landau was driving slowly into Applegarth, its perfectly matched team of chestnuts driven by Harry Parr. Inside the closed carriage sat Lady Amelia.

With a sinking heart, Jessica waited for the knock upon the door. She heard the tap-tapping of the old lady's stick and then the pearl handle was struck once against the yellow door, a peremptory sound that grated on Jessica.

She opened the door and looked coldly at Lady Amelia. "Good day, my lady."

"Miss Durleigh."

I shall not ask you in, thought Jessica, staying where she was and waiting.

"Your manners are as appalling as your morals, Miss Durleigh, for you surely do not wish Parr to hear what we have to say."

"Please come in, my lady."

Lady Amelia looked around the kitchen, scraping her toe on the freshly-raddled floor and sniffing as she viewed the row of hoggins and the strings of onions hanging from the beams. "How charming," she murmured, and Jessica took a long breath to quell her anger.

"And how may I help you, Lady Amelia?"

"In two ways." The old lady's shrewd little eyes were taking note of everything, as if she sought something in particular.

Suddenly Jessica guessed one of the reasons for the visit. "You are actually wondering if

Sir Nicholas is here with me!" She laughed.

Lady Amelia's wrinkled face went pale with anger and then two spots of color shone on her cheeks. "I cannot see your reason for such uproarious laughter."

"Can't you? Well, perhaps that does not surprise me. But let me assure you, madam, that no one by the name of Woodville is welcome here. You and your son are almost equally abhorrent, but perhaps you have the edge."

"Quite the sharp-tongued miss, aren't we? Well, I shall do my utmost to wipe the smile from your face, Miss Durleigh. I was informed my daughter-in-law had been seen on the Padbury road with Varangian this morning. I conclude that they intend marrying there, now that Henbury will have nothing to do with them. I will not have it, Miss Durleigh. She will *not* marry another man."

"And how will you prevent it? She is a free agent."

"Is she? Well, perhaps she is, Miss Durleigh, but Varangian is not. Oh, I don't mean he has a wife secreted away somewhere. I mean that his life is not his to do with as he pleases. And I mean to see that he remembers the fact."

"I don't understand."

The old lady smiled, drawing her gloved fingers along a shelf and glancing at the dark kid to see if there was dust. "Do you not? Well, that does not matter. What does matter is that you are continuing to give her shelter and I do not like that. She is Philip's wife."

"Widow."

"She is still his, no matter what, and I will not

suffer her to behave so irreverently. She must return to Woodville House."

"I will not force her."

"Then I will ruin Varangian."

Jessica stared, her mind racing. "How?"

"It lies in my power, that should suffice."

The note! Surely it could only be that. "I begin to see clearly, Lady Amelia, from where Philip got his more unpleasant side. So, you now intend carrying on where he left the reins dangling?"

"Varangian holds his estates illegally, Miss Durleigh, so it is only right that he should pay for the pleasure."

"Is that how you see it? That Francis should pay blood money to you and your dead son? If you are so concerned with the right and wrong of Francis' tenure of the estates, why then did you not send the note to Ireland, to seek out any relatives of the dead man, O'Connor?"

"You know that much do you?"

"I know enough to find myself thoroughly revolted by you and by what I now know of Philip."

The old woman flushed angrily. "I do not care how you feel, Miss Durleigh, for I am intent upon destroying this affair of Rosamund's. And believe me, I will use all the irons in the fire in order to do so. Philip's name shall be protected and his memory cherished. I am determined, and I *shall* succeed, even if it means turning Varangian from his lands."

"And what is my part to be in this grand plan?"

"Turn Rosamund out."

"She will go to Francis."

"No. For he, by then, will know that the price

199

of Varangian is the casting off of Rosamund Woodville. She is a Woodville now, Miss Durleigh, and she will always remain so."

"You are quite mad. Evil and mad. And if I tell Nicholas what you are doing?" She was prepared to try any path through this maze.

"Nicholas would not listen to you, and besides, no one appears to know where he is."

"You do not seem particularly concerned about him."

"He is his own master." Lady Amelia turned, her hand on the door. "There is just one last thing, Miss Durleigh. I have yet another desire in all this. Francis Varangian will also lose his estates if *you* do not sell this property to me. I am prepared to offer you a fair price. But I must have you out of Henbury, for you are a reminder to the world that my son kept a mistress. That he was driven by his love for you into forgetting his wife and his obligations."

"How quaint a picture you paint of Philip, Lady Amelia, I had no idea you were so accomplished an artist. So deftly do you use the brush it is impossible to see the flaws on the canvas."

"There will be no flaws when I am finished, Miss Durleigh. No flaws at all. Philip will be as he was before he met you."

"He will be as *you* wish to see him."

"My terms are stated. You must leave Applegarth, and Rosamund must return to Woodville House. That way, Francis Varangian keeps his fortune. Otherwise, I will destroy him. You will not lose by complying, for with the price I give you, you may purchase a property in an area more suited to you."

"I cannot sell. I must stay here for two years."

"I can buy it from you, Miss Durleigh. Have no fear of that, for the will was specific. The Woodville family could purchase the property from you. I would have done so earlier, but Nicholas would not agree. I do not think he will prevent the sale this time, though, for he has recovered from his momentary lapse of sanity where you are concerned. But Philip shall rise unstained from all this, madam, and make no mistake about it. He knew that Rosamund loved Varangian, you know, that's why he did it."

"Did what?"

"Put the restrictions upon your tenure of Applegarth. He told me he wished to guard against his sudden death releasing Rosamund. He deliberately left you a small income and Applegarth, knowing that when you came back to Henbury, Francis Varangian would turn to you again. At least, he believed that would be the case, but it seems we were wrong there, for Varangian did not, after all, show an interest in you. But I am about to put all that right. It was Philip's wish, and I will do all in my considerable power to honor his wish."

Jessica felt sick. "Good day, Lady Amelia."

"Good day, Miss Durleigh."

Chapter 24

When Rosamund returned from Padbury with Francis, Jessica could say nothing of what had happened. She saw how happy they both were—even Francis, who was still worried about the note—and she could not say the words that would destroy that happiness.

"Jess, we are to be married in two weeks' time at Padbury." Rosamund seized her hands warmly, her eyes shining with happiness.

"I am glad."

Francis kissed Jessica's cheek. "I cannot thank you enough for giving Rosamund your aid in all this."

Tears filled her eyes at these words. What should she do? How could she say what Lady Amelia had said? She stood there in miserable indecision, when a pony and trap rattled to the door and Tamsin got down. She was with Harry Parr and looked excited.

"Miss Jess, Sir Nicholas is found!"

"Oh."

"Yes. He were locked away by Jamie Pike, so they say. It be a real mystery, for I thought Jamie got clean away, but it do seem as he was in Henbury all the time."

"And is Sir Nicholas well?"

"Reckon so. He looked mortal tired and hungry when I saw him, though."

"Saw him?"

"Aye. I were visiting with Harry here."

"Good evening, Mr. Parr."

"Good evening, Miss Durleigh."

"And are you fully recovered now?"

"Yes. And that's why I've brought Tamsin out here afore the wagonette left, to say my thanks to you for helping me that night."

"I did not do much."

"Still, I thought I'd say my piece."

"Thank you. Will you not take some refreshment, for I am sure Tamsin would be pleased to drink a glass of wine with you."

"Elderberry?" he asked, his eyes brightening.

Tamsin frowned. "Mind your manners, Harry Parr, for this be Miss Durleigh's house and she don't serve no common elderberry. Madeira be what you'm offered."

"Thank you kindly then. I'd like some."

Jessica turned, for Francis was taking his leave. The moment had passed and she had said nothing. And now there were too many people. Perhaps, if she were to say nothing, if she was to wait and hope, then Lady Amelia would change her mind. But it was a faint hope.

She was so distracted she had no appetite, and Tamsin bundled her to bed early, fearing her to be sickening from some malady. A cup of hot caudle was placed resolutely by the bedside.

"And if I comes up here in five minutes and you've not drunk that, then I shall have something to say, Miss Jess!"

"Yes, Tamsin." Jessica lay quietly in bed, looking with distaste at the steaming cup. She sat up and forced herself to drink it, although her stomach was churning and she felt horribly cold and unwell. How could she do what Lady Amelia wished? How could she destroy the happiness of two people who were so much in love? She knew, intuitively, that Francis would not choose Rosamund, for to do that would be to bring ignominy upon his dead father's name. And it would bring Rosamund into a life of destitution and infamy, for the scandal Lady Amelia would set in motion would spread the length and breadth of England. Francis would never do that to the woman he loved; he would cast her off first. And Lady Amelia would have her way.

"Ah, you've drunk it all down. There now, you have a good rest and happen you'll feel better in the morning."

"Yes, Tamsin. Tamsin?"

"Yes, Miss Jess?"

"Did you speak to Sir Nicholas?"

"I should say so. I'd a lot to say and all!"

Jessica closed her eyes faintly. "What did you say?"

"Enough. But it were like water off a duck's back. He merely bowed and thanked me for my concern. That's all he said. I could have been felled with a feather, so I could."

"Was he all right?"

"Ah, Jamie locked him in the hurdle hut over by the lake. He, I mean, Sir Nicholas, didn't say why, or anything like that. Just that it were Jamie."

When the door closed again Jessica looked at the mulberry hangings of the bed. Why had Jamie gone to see Nicholas? Why had he left the safety of Ladywood to risk being seen in the lanes around Henbury?

Her head was aching; there had been so many unpleasantnesses in this most hateful of days. And this was all because Lady Amelia wished the world to remember Philip Woodville with kindness. His name must be shielded from all calumny.

If only the truth could be spread as certainly. Jessica would have loved to have struck back at the wicked, old woman. But how? That was the question. If the world could only know how Philip had blackmailed poor Francis. But Francis would not admit to the world that he had paid such sums to Philip. Her eyes followed the golden tassels and rested on the carved bed. If she could make Lady Amelia believe that Francis would take Philip with him into perdition, that would surely make her change her mind. But Francis would not give her a letter as proof to use as a lever, she knew that. She sat up then. Of course! Mr. Slade's little book, with its carefully written pages. It stated there quite clearly that Philip had paid for the necklace with money from Francis. What if she could persuade Lady Amelia that Francis intended making it known that Philip *stole* the money? What price Philip's good name then?

Jessica threw back the coverlets and stood. Her eyes were shining now. There was a good chance it might work. Lady Amelia would surely pause to consider if such a threat were issued. A counterthreat. Tit for tat. The fact that Francis had no such intention was not important—it was that Lady Amelia would believe it to be true.

She glanced at the window. The evening was drawing in slightly, but there was still sunlight. She would go to Woodville House tonight and beard the lion in its den.

"Tamsin?"

The door at the foot of the stairs opened and Tamsin hurried up. "What be wrong, Miss Jess?"

"Nothing's wrong. Nothing at all. Now, I am going to Woodville House and I wish to look my finest. My hair must be perfect, and my clothes exactly right."

"Now?"

"Yes. I dare not wait until morning." Jessica was thinking that the old lady might choose any moment to fire her first salvo at Francis.

"But you'm not well, lovey. You should bide in bed tonight. And why go there?"

"There is something I must do. Now, will you help me dress, or must I do everything myself?"

"I'll help you, Miss Jess, don't fret. What shall you wear?"

"My finest London toggery. I want to make an impression on the old dragon."

"Oh, then 'tis Lady Amelia you're out to see?"

"Yes. Now, I think my jade pelisse, and the flounced, oyster lawn. No, the brown spencer and the oyster lawn. Yes, that would do very well. And the straw bonnet with the orchids. Brown gloves and slippers, and my dark-brown reticule."

"Smart togs, right enough. But why have you to impress the old one?"

"I'll not answer that, Tamsin."

"Well, 'tis your business, I reckon." Tamsin picked up the hairbrush and took off Jessica's mobcap. The chestnut hair tumbled down in unruly curls that the brush set briskly about.

In a short while Jessica was at last buttoning the tight, high-waisted spencer, and surveying her reflection in the mirror. Yes, she would do well enough, she decided. She straightened the bonnet and fluffed out the creamy ribbons until they looked just right. The velvet orchids bobbed slightly below the brim of the bonnet, resting against her hair in a cluster of oyster and bronze petals. The old she-cat would not have seen such London finery for many a day.

Downstairs, Rosamund looked at her in amazement. "You are going out?"

"Yes."

"Is that why Tamsin is getting the dogcart ready?"

"Yes."

"But where are you going?"

"To visit your mother-in-law." Jessica undid the parcel containing Mr. Slade's book. Only one page did she need. She flicked through the book until she found what she wanted, and she ripped out the page carefully. "I'm sorry, Mr. Slade, but this matter is more important than your little book's pristine state."

"Whatever do you mean?"

"Nothing. Nothing at all. Ah, Tamsin has brought Jinks around to the front." Jessica folded the piece of paper and put it in her reticule.

She took the reins from Tamsin who looked disapproving. "This ain't right, Miss Jess, driving out at this hour, and to such a place, and all."

"I will not be long, Tamsin." Jessica slapped the reins and Jinks clattered busily out of Applegarth and onto the Henbury road. Her heart was thundering nervously, and she found her hands were soon damp in the kid gloves. But she was determined this ruse would work, for if it did not. . . . She slapped the reins again and brought Jinks up to a merry pace.

A horseman emerged from the woods by Applegarth. Rosamund saw him from the kitchen window. "Oh, dear, Nicholas is coming."

"And not before time, neither!" Tamsin wiped her hands on her apron and opened the door. "Good evening, Sir Nicholas."

He dismounted. "Good evening, Miss Davey. Is Miss Durleigh in?"

"No, you've missed her by not more than half an hour."

He slapped his gloves against his thigh. "And when will she return, for I must see her."

"To put things right?" demanded Tamsin determinedly.

He smiled. "Yes. I came as soon as I had washed and eaten, for I could not have come as I was, could I?"

"Reckon not. But happen I don't know if she wants to see you now, she'm proper bad about it all."

"With good reason, I fear." He looked beyond the countrywoman to where Rosamund sat in the kitchen. "Rosamund?"

She stood. "Nicholas."

He pushed his gloves into his hat and stepped inside, holding out his hand. "I believe congratulations are in order."

Hesitantly, she took the proffered hand. "I did not think you would wish to congratulate us, Nicholas."

"Bygones are bygones, Rosamund. You have chosen Francis, and he seems of a like lunacy concerning you, so I am happy enough to wish you well."

She smiled then. "Thank you." She still held his hand. "But Lady Amelia. . . ."

"My mother will bow to the inevitable. Even she will do that."

"Do you think so? She made certain that we cannot marry in Henbury."

His eyes sharpened. "She did what?"

"She 'persuaded' the vicar of St. Mary's not to perform any wedding ceremony for us."

"The devil she did. Then I'll 'unpersuade' him for you. She has no right to do that, especially not over my repulsive brother. Leave my mother to me, for she knows who is master of Woodville House."

"Perhaps it would be best to leave matters as

they are, for we are now to marry at Padbury."

"Foreign land? My sister-in-law will marry in Henbury, or I'll know the reason why. Tell me, how is Jessica? Do you think I've muffed my chances there?"

"I don't know, Nicholas, and that is the truth. She was very unhappy I know. But now she conceals her thoughts and does not confide in either Tamsin or myself. She is either over you completely, or so in love with you still that it hurts to mention your name. I am not sure which."

"Then I must pray for the latter possibility, must I not?"

"But why did you do it to her? Why?"

"Because, damn it, I was jealous! I thought her to have a fancy for Jamie Pike. Jealousy curls you inside, Rosamund, as you of all people must know."

She smiled. "Oh, I know. But at least I had cause, for Francis did indeed love her at one time, enough to have asked her to marry him. But you had no such cause to be jealous."

"I see that now, but at the time I was inclined to be unreasonable. Where is she now?"

"She has driven to Woodville House, to see Lady Amelia."

He looked surprised. "To see my mother? What about?"

"I don't know. She wouldn't tell us. But she got from her bed and dressed like ten, new-minted pennies."

He pulled on his gloves and hat. "I think perhaps my presence over there might be useful, don't you?"

"I think so, too."

211

Chapter 25

"Miss Durleigh." The butler's voice was round in the quiet room.

Lady Amelia sat by the fire, her black crepe gown catching the soft glow. Her eyes shone. "Ah, Miss Durleigh, so you have come with a decision?"

"No." Jessica watched as the butler closed the heavy door.

"Then why are you here?"

"Because I think, madam, that we must bargain."

"I think not, missy. I think not."

"Then you must take the consequences, my lady. And I think you will find they will make null and void all your careful groundwork."

The claw-like hands moved on the pearl handle. "I don't take your meaning, Miss Durleigh."

"Philip will be much maligned."

"And what could *you* do, missy? How could *you* touch him? Eh?"

"It is not I who will do it, my lady, it is Francis Varangian. You see, he will fight. And as you have chosen to take off the gloves for this bout, then he will do the same."

"Indeed?" The old lady leaned forward to tug at a bell pull. "Ah, Tanner, some black coffee, if you please. And you, Miss Durleigh?"

"No, thank you." I will not take your hospitality, you she-cat, thought Jessica.

"For one then, Tanner."

The butler bowed and closed the doors once more. Lady Amelia looked at Jessica. "And what, pray, does Varangian have in mind?"

"Proof that Philip took money from him."

The old woman smiled. "You mean me to believe that Varangian would voluntarily admit to having been blackmailed."

"I see you do not shrink to name your crime, my lady. But no, I do not speak of blackmail. I said 'took' as in steal, thieve, misappropriate, and similar words."

The smile faded. "Philip stole nothing of Varangian's."

"That is not what Francis will say. The word he will use will be clear to all who choose to listen. He will claim Philip stole a large sum of money with which to purchase a diamond necklace. And the proof of this lies with the jeweler who was commissioned to make the necklace."

The room was very quiet. Jessica could hear the slow ticking of the glass-cased clock on the mantelpiece.

"But it is not true."

"Who will believe that, when the world and his wife knew how Philip was? You cannot disguise him, Lady Amelia. He made himself clear to all and sundry. With two noticeable exceptions—and we now look at each other across this fire."

"You loved him, Miss Durleigh?"

"Why else would I have done what I did? I left considerably more luxury in a marriage with Francis than I ever hoped to enjoy by living with Philip. My motives, therefore, could not be said to be mercenary. I went with him because I loved him, yes."

"And now you are determined there shall be more odium heaped upon his name?"

"I am determined to stop you, my lady. And if I can do so, I will. But Francis does not need my persuasion in this. He is determined to fight back, as you will find to your cost if you persist."

"Is this for Rosamund then?"

"He loves her and she has always loved him. There is no sin in that, for even Philip himself never pretended to have any affection for her. That is something else the world and his wife knows."

"The world and his wife would appear to have almost a vested interest in the outcome of this struggle, Miss Durleigh," remarked Lady Amelia dryly. "You know, I had hardly considered that you must have loved him. How strange it should not have occurred to me. However, I digress. The matter in hand is this diamond necklace that appears to be somewhat pertinent now. You have not come here merely to inform me of Varangian's threat, have you, Miss Durleigh? Pray explain further, if you please."

"I have in mind what, as children, we called 'swaps.'"

"*Swaps?*" The aristocratic lips curled a little.

Unflustered, Jessica continued. "Yes, the proof concerning the necklace—which is the page from the jeweler's book—for the note you have in your possession."

"Ah." Lady Amelia stood, leaning on her stick. "Why are you intent upon this, Miss Durleigh? What reason could you have for wishing to interfere?"

"You involved me, and you chose to pressure me into leaving Henbury."

"On my own head be it?"

"Yes."

"And if I withdraw my wish concerning your tenure at Applegarth? If I leave you entirely alone? What then?"

Jessica shook her head. "No. I would still be here as I now am, offering a swap that would end the matter once and for all. I am sure, Lady Amelia, that you do not really wish to have Rosamund here when she would despise you. She could, if she wished, make Philip's name even more reviled than it is. She has only to constantly speak of him to insure that. But if she marries Francis, then she would not even think of Philip. Your own name, too, would be in her hands. Surely, you see that? Rosamund loves Francis far too much to accept your will meekly."

"I see your influence upon her there, Miss Durleigh, for she was a submissive, mild, genteel young lady before you returned."

Jessica smiled. "My influence still has her a pure, young woman who has done nothing blameworthy. Had she her own way, she would by now be living sinfully at Varangian Hall. Now, about my offer."

"I do not believe Varangian will use the matter of the necklace."

Standing, Jessica shook her skirts and shrugged. "The choice is yours, and the consequences will lie upon you and you alone. Good evening, Lady Amelia." She began to walk to the door.

"Miss Durleigh. Please. Sit down." The old lady looked at her, turning her head as the door opened and the butler brought in the silver tray with a coffee pot and crockery. When he had gone she sat down. "Will you pour for me, please, for my hands are no longer steady."

Jessica lifted the elegant coffee pot and poured the thick dark liquid into a fine porcelain cup.

"Miss Durleigh, I am forced to consider your offer. But I must know if the paper in your possession is the only copy."

"Yes, it is. Mrs. Slade especially asked for the book's return, as it is his only record."

"How dishonest of Varangian to remove a page from such a book. Or is it Varangian? I rather suspect, Miss Durleigh, that young Francis has had nothing to do with this. That it is you who have perpetrated the matter. I can well imagine you tearing a page from the book, but not Varangian."

"I am the culprit. But Francis would still charge Philip with theft."

"Perhaps he would. I believe he would not. But, it is a risk which I am not prepared to take if you are involved, as obviously you are—heart and soul. You would, no doubt, eventually influ-

217

ence him to do your will, and Rosamund would support you with some alacrity." The old lady sipped the coffee, her bright eyes looking at Jessica in the firelight. "I will agree, Miss Durleigh. Let Rosamund have Varangian, and let him have his estates. I am not willing to embark upon a fight with you and with my son, and with Rosamund and with Varangian. The odds have become a little too steep for me."

Relief swept through Jessica and she tried desperately to hide it. "It is surely the best way all round."

"No doubt, you think so. But you knew Philip—can you not see why I have tried to fight for him like this?" The proud, old woman was suddenly a mother speaking of a much-loved son. Her eyes were soft and Jessica thought she could see tears glistening as she looked up at his portrait.

"I loved him very much, my lady. I gave up everything for him, and he made me very happy, as I believe I made him happy, too. My return to Somerset has seen the shattering of my illusions, and it has been a painful experience, I do assure you. To find that the man you loved so inordinately was, in every way, despised and hated by all who knew him, and to find the crimes of which he was responsible, and the vices in which he indulged. Rosamund has told me much that I will not speak of to anyone, not even to you. But I saw nothing of his dark side. To me he was always gentle, loving, and kind."

A tear wended its way down the wrinkled cheek. "He was always thus, Miss Durleigh. An unpredictable mixture—sometimes effervescent and sparkling, sometimes dour and black. I saw it in

218

him as a child; he was an enigma. He could have been great, but the darkness came over him too often. Perhaps it was as well that he died when he did, for surely a terrible nemesis would have been waiting. He could not have gone on. I have never spoken like this of him to anyone before."

"But I understand how you feel. Perhaps I am the only other person who understands so well."

Lady Amelia nodded. "This little key opens the drawer in that writing cabinet, Miss Durleigh. Inside you will find a casket. Please bring it to me."

Jessica obeyed, and placed the casket in the old woman's hands. From a chain around her neck Lady Amelia drew another key with which she opened the casket. Inside lay a single, folded sheet of paper. "This is what you wish to have, Miss Durleigh—the cause of all the trouble."

Opening her reticule, Jessica took out the page from Mr. Slade's book.

Lady Amelia glanced over it, nodding. "Yes, it was a well thought plan, Miss Durleigh, but one which I think would not have withstood a court of law."

"Perhaps not, but the mud would cling a little, would it not?"

"And you know all too well how mud lingers, do you not? Will you do something for me now, Miss Durleigh? Will you help me to burn both of these documents? Then we shall know that all is indeed accomplished."

Together they dropped the papers onto the fire and Jessica pushed them into the glowing heart with a poker. They curled and blackened, wisps drawn up the chimney by the draft and heat.

Soon there was nothing to be seen of them.

"And how will our lives touch from now on?" asked the older woman suddenly.

"They will not. There is no reason why they should." Jessica looked away quickly.

"I was referring to my son, Nicholas."

"No. You need not concern yourself that there is anything between us."

"I do not concern myself, at least not in the way you hint at. I admire a woman who is so loyal to her friends. Such people are gem stones, Miss Durleigh."

Jessica stood. "There is still nothing between Nicholas and me. It begins to grow dark now and I must drive back."

"You know that you are welcome here, Miss Durleigh."

"So complete a *volte-face?*"

"And why not? I think we understand each other and respect each other now."

"Yes, I think we do."

"Perhaps you should tell Rosamund that if she wishes to return here and to go to her wedding from here as my daughter-in-law, then she, too, is more than welcome. If we are to set the past behind us, then I think we must do so completely. There must be no loose ends to entangle the future."

"I will tell her. Good night, Lady Amelia."

"Good night, Miss Durleigh."

Chapter 26

"Jessica?"

She turned, holding Jinks' bridle. Nicholas walked from the stables, across the driveway to where she stood. "Sir Nicholas."

"I came as soon as I knew where you were."

"You need not have concerned yourself, sir." She quelled the tumultuous longing which seized her at seeing him again. It was all finished—he had made that abundantly clear.

"Why did you wish to see my mother?"

"That, sir, is surely my business."

He stiffened. "Assuredly it is, Miss Durleigh. Shall I accompany you back to Applegarth, for darkness will soon be upon us?"

"There is no need."

"Damn it, I *want* to!" he snapped.

"Do not raise your voice to me, sir, for I am not one of your lackeys."

He nodded. "With that remark I will agree, and I apologize for having raised my voice. I apologize, too, for my unforgivable behavior in the recent past. I have since been thoroughly convinced of the error of my ways."

Her hands were trembling, and Jinks shook his head free of her, shuffling his feet slightly. "I don't understand."

"You surely have heard of my ignominious capture and imprisonment by Jamie Pike? I had imagined the whole of Henbury was ringing with the tale."

"I had heard, yes."

"His purpose was to set the record in order, concerning you, Jessica."

"Oh, Jamie." She looked away.

"I can still feel jealous when you say his name so softly." He reached out to take her hand. "Can you find it in your heart to forgive me?"

Could she? The hurt had run deep. But when she looked at him she knew that she loved him and wanted him. She nodded. "I can forgive you, for I love you. You know that I do."

He drew her closer, untying the ribbons of her bonnet and tossing it onto the dogcart. Twining his fingers in her thick hair he pulled her face to meet his in a kiss that was long and gentle. "And I love you, Jess," he murmured.

She held him tightly, her eyes shining with happiness. How this day had changed, swinging her from the depths of despair to the heights of joy.

He saw a movement in the window behind and saw his mother standing there. She smiled at him and turned away. His arms tightened around Jessica. "What spell have you cast over my formidable mother?"

"No spell. We understand each other, that is all."

"Jess, have you forgotten my brother now? Is he completely in the past?"

"Yes."

"So, it is Nicholas Woodville you embrace now, not the ghost of Philip?"

She looked at him. "How could you think that? My anguish at thinking I lost you was proof enough of my love for you. I thought my heart would break."

"I was a jealous boor, and do not deserve a second chance." He kissed her again. "And so I will not muff it this time. Will you marry me, Jess?"

She stared. *"Marry* you? But I am not a suitable wife for you, Nicholas. Not with my past so well known by everyone."

"I love you and I want you. You shall be Lady Woodville, for I am set upon it. Will you marry me?"

She closed her eyes, nodding. "Yes."

He laughed, swinging her into the air. "Henbury church bells are going to be worn out shortly, with three weddings to celebrate."

"Three?"

"Yes. Ours. Rosamund and Francis. And Tamsin Davey and Harry Parr."

"I had no idea."

"Harry told me this morning that he intends asking her. I was thinking—you'll not need Applegarth now, will you?"

She smiled, kissing him. "It will make a fine wedding gift for them," she murmured. "And I have a necklace for Rosamund," she added.